# LUCY ZEEZOU'S GOAL

## LIZ DEEP-JONES

# LUCY ZEEZOU'S GOAL

## LIZ DEEP-JONES

First published in 2008 by Random House.
Second Edition published in 2023 by Popcorn Press,
the fiction imprint of Fair Play Publishing
PO Box 4101, Balgowlah Heights, NSW 2093, Australia
www.popcornpress.com.au

ISBN: 978-1-925914-80-1
ISBN: 978-1-925914-81-8 (ePub)
© Liz Deep-Jones 2008, 2023



Front cover photograph by Tim Bauer
Model Izabella Deep-Jones
Cover design and typesetting by Ana Secivanovic

All inquiries should be made to the Publisher via sales@fairplaypublishing.com.au

# DEDICATION

*To my extraordinary parents, the late, David and Jeanette Deep.*

*I'm living my dream, sharing stories as a journalist*
*and writer because of their unwavering belief*
*and support in all my endeavours.*

*I'm so grateful for their unconditional love and inspiring me*
*to be fearless and live my life to the fullest.*

*My dreams continue ...*

'This is a book for kids which features a young girl who is passionate about football. You can't help but love Lucy. She's a character that rings true for anyone aspiring to be a professional footballer just like me. An imaginative and exciting story for everyone with a dream.'

*Paolo Maldini, Former AC Milan and Italy National team*

'It's great to read a book that shows you can achieve your dreams no matter what. I'm glad the next generation of footballers has Lucy Zeezou to look up to.'

*Melissa Barbieri, former Matildas captain and goalkeeper*

'I wish there was a book like this when I was a kid, Lucy Zeezou's Goal is an exciting story with a great mix of football and fashion.'

*Dianne Alagich, former Matilda*

'It is inspiring to follow Lucy's trials and tribulations as she pursues her footballing dream with such passion and gusto. A must read.'

*Clare Hunt, Matilda*

'This is a captivating story! Lucy is an infectious character, fearless in the pursuit of her dream. Love it!'

*Craig Foster AM, former Socceroo*

'Liz has written a book which is ideal for all girls chasing their dream just like it's engaging character, Lucy. The story is a magical mix of football and fashion which is captivating and inspirational. Lucy Zeezou's Goal is a must read.'

*Tom Sermanni, former Head Coach of the Matildas*

# CONTENTS

# Chapter 1

# The Penalty

The whistle blew . . . I was taken down inside the box and it didn't look good. A rough tackle from behind sent me flying through the air and crashing down to the ground, right in front of the referee.

I looked up and saw the crowd on their feet, gasping. I shook my head and took a second look, but it really was true: I was playing in front of a packed house on my dream pitch. I couldn't believe my luck as I looked around, trying to take in the electric atmosphere at the famous San Siro stadium. It was really me, Lucy Zeezou, right there on the field. The fans had been chanting and cheering.

And then to add to my excitement a player wearing the same jersey yelled out with concern and raced over to help me. 'Lucy, Lucy, are you all right?'

'Um . . . I've never been better,' I replied with the biggest smile I could muster.

Oh my goodness, it was my hero, retired football legend Zinedine Zidane, famously known as Zizou. I was nicknamed Zeezou after Zidane himself – a nickname I carried with pride. Zidane was a master of the game. I loved the way he played and dominated the midfield. He was a magician with the ball – just mesmerising.

This was unbelievable! Around eighty thousand football fans in my hometown of Milan, Italy, were watching this game between some of the best male and female players on earth – stars including retired US legend Mia Hamm, Australia's Cheryl Salisbury, Lionel Messi, Ronaldinho, Kaká, Cristiano Ronaldo, David Beckham and . . . *me*! I was in heaven, playing in the same team as all these stars, including my namesake, in a mixed World XI side against Italy's best male and female stars.

The referee awarded our team a penalty, which might be the last kick of the match. To make the situation even more surreal, Zidane said, 'Lucy, you take this penalty.'

I was dumbstruck. I was surrounded by the world's best and he believed that I could kick the winning goal.

I could feel the pressure mounting. My stomach was churning and my right shooting leg hurt but I was more determined than ever to succeed. I *would* convert this penalty to lift the winner's trophy with my revered team mates and follow the family tradition of my late grandpa, Nonno Dino, and my papa, both football legends in Italy. Nonno Dino was my greatest supporter. He passed away a year ago after a sudden heart attack. He believed in me and knew that one day I would make it. I wished he was here to see me.

I looked up and watched the clock ticking away, a reminder that this was it. It felt as if something great was about to happen. My heart pumped like a pounding drum but I had to stay calm and treat this kick like any other.

The arena fell eerily silent, I took a few deep breaths as the referee blew his whistle and I took my run up to the ball. Make this and I'd be a hero, miss it and I'd be the villain. I wanted to show Papa that I could do it, that I was capable of being a top footballer.

I struck the ball, injecting life into it as it hurtled towards the goal. I followed the ball's path through the air as it climbed – floating, spiralling, and then heading towards the back of the net.

Suddenly my perfect moment was interrupted by the invasive sounds of clicking and shouting. A hand grabbed my shoulder.

# Chapter 2

# Cover girl

'Lucia? Luuucia . . . hello?'

I was startled into an upright position, and looked around with great surprise as the football pitch I was playing on had disappeared. Instead, I was facing an old family friend, Enzo Galliano, one of Italy's most sought after photographers. I was sitting on a comfy lounge in his plush photographic studio overlooking the familiar cobblestoned streets of Milan. To make matters worse, I wasn't in my football kit, but dressed up like a Barbie doll, with drops of sweat rolling down my face.

'Oh, sorry, I must have dozed off,' I mumbled. I desperately wanted to close my eyes again to see if I scored the winning goal, but Enzo was on a mission. Reality sucked!

'I only went out for about ten minutes to grab a few more lights from my storeroom and I found you asleep on the lounge. It was hard to wake you, but,' he insisted, 'we must press on with the shoot.'

I still felt drowsy and shook my head in an attempt to bring myself back to the land of the living.

'You don't look as though you're quite with us. This is no time to sleep, Lucia. You must be fresh and alert. Your make-up needs freshening up, too.'

He called Anastasia, the hair and make-up artist, and she came running in with her kit. 'Oh, Lucia, you really look zapped. This will make you feel better.' She began gently touching up my make-up. A few more dabs with the powder puff and I was ready to face the camera.

'Look into the lens and smile . . . that's it! Now chin up, throw your head back, and I want to see more of that fabulous long blonde hair. That's better! Lovely, Lucia, now you're working the camera,' Enzo encouraged.

Oh, great, lovely! NOT! Click, click, click. I was sick of this posing business. Mama had dragged me to another photoshoot, this time for the cover of an Italian teen magazine called *Dieci*, which means ten. I suppose most girls would love to be on the cover of a magazine, posing for the camera, but this was what Mama wanted, not me. She thought it was in my best interest, the path to a lucrative, exciting career. Sure it was fun being pampered and stuff, but it was too superficial for my liking.

Just because Mama's modelling career didn't work out as she'd hoped, she'd been pushing me to live her dream. She was well known in Australia before I was born – she was on the cover of lots of magazines, featured in commercials and even acted in some films, but she didn't really make it on the international stage.

While chasing a career in Europe she was swept off her feet by my papa at a famous disco in Milan called Hollywood. It was a popular hangout for many of Italy's top footballers, international models and actors. And so Mama fell in love, gave up full-time modelling and married Papa. As the glamorous wife of a famous Italian football star, Mama fitted right in. And these days she was in her element running a successful fashion business called 23, which kept her and Papa extremely busy.

'Lucia, look this way. Great! Now a little twirl. That's lovely, sweetie,' shouted Enzo.

This was getting more and more frustrating – all I wanted to do was play football, not perform another little twirl . . . Mama would kill me if she knew I'd been skipping dance class and casting sessions just to play football. My little trick was to tell our driver to take the rest of the day off so I could do my own thing. The less people knew about my secret, the better.

Luckily, in my neighbourhood, Brera, which is pretty much in the centre of Milan, everything was within walking distance. As soon as school finished, I'd race off to football at the park just up the road, missing my dance lessons at the studio around the corner. Thankfully I lived just five minutes away so it had been a doddle. I'd got away with it for the past year, since my parents banned me from playing football. It was a good thing they were always too busy to attend any dance concerts, or anything else I did for that matter.

I'd tried to tell them I'd rather be out on the pitch kicking the ball and trying to crack one into the back of the net, but they never seemed to hear me. I think they assumed it was a phase I'd grow out of, like a little kid. But I wasn't so little. I was fourteen years old, tall for my age and ready to kick butt. No matter what it took, I was going to find a way to follow my dream. So in order to keep playing football after they banned me, I had no choice but to lead a secret football life.

Enzo brought me back to earth. 'One more twirl. Perfect! Okay, Lucia, it's a wrap!'

My parents named me Lucia Zoffi but my friends called me Lucy because Mama was Australian and Lucy was the Australian version of my name. I preferred being called Lucy, and it was definitely much better than Skippy. That was another thing I battled with my parents about: they absolutely refused to call me Lucy. How would they feel if I just called them Frida and Paolo?

I grew up in Milano, as we say in Italy. Papa was born here, a buzzing city where everyone is obsessed with football *and* fashion. For football fans – which is nearly everyone – the game is more than a national sport . . . it is a way of life! To the Milanese, the city reigns supreme, thanks to the dominance of its two premier football teams. AC Milan and Inter Milan are fierce rivals. Even though they share the same stadium, they divide the city with their passionate supporters. Controversial referee decisions can spark arguments between families that last for weeks. The game's a religion.

The style-conscious come here to be enchanted too, as Milan's one of the world's leading fashion capitals alongside Paris, London and New York. The Milanese parade around in impeccable designer outfits, looking as though they've just stepped off the catwalk, even if they're just off to the supermarket. It was easy to see why Mama fell in love with the place. Mama revelled in everything Milan had to offer. It was a far cry from her humble upbringing in Sydney's Kings Cross.

Her dream to make it in Europe kind of came true – and to be fair, she did more than just lunch. She was the face of her own women's wear collection, and the driving force of the company she ran with Papa. He also enjoyed the fashion scene and loved to watch the parades when he got a chance, but for now Mama ran the show. The company was a big part of Papa's retirement plan.

Thanks to their successful business and Papa's status as a god in Italy, Mama was good friends with all the top designers. Her dressing room was full of their clothes and when she had a special event she usually had a one-off designer piece made. Heaven forbid she get caught in the same outfit as another celebrity.

And yes, Mama was pushy. She insisted that I parade along the catwalk at her friends' charity fashion events while she beamed alongside me. I'd been doing it for so long I didn't really get nervous walking out into the spotlight . . . I just took it in my stride, even though I'd always been a little clumsy. I was always tripping over or walking into something. Maybe it was because I had a tendency to drift off into my own world when I got bored.

I tried to make sure I had a bit of fun with the whole experience. Depending on my mood, I'd sometimes pretend to be someone else. I loved acting like the singer Pink. She's a rebel, a cheeky, strong-minded woman. She says what she thinks no matter what's at stake. Acting like that, I didn't feel so bad about being dressed up in clothes I wasn't into.

Needless to say, strutting my stuff on the catwalk had been a mixed bag of fun and calamity, especially when I had to don high heels – they were so not my thing.

At a recent event one of the designers was outraged when I refused to wear stilettos especially made to match the gown. Instead, I snuck on my old sneakers and playfully skipped along the catwalk in front of a full house of celebrities, fashion industry types and the media. I did the Pink thing and got carried away. But then I somehow tripped over the gown because of its silly long tail. I felt everyone freeze, but I quickly popped up with a dance move and continued on my way.

The designer and Mama looked on in horror but the crowd seemed to enjoy it – they must have thought it was part of the show, because I got a round of applause from the front-row celebrities, and the photographers were happily snapping away at my cheeky looks.

The designer had no choice but to forgive me, thanks to the overwhelming support – although backstage it was a different story. I heard a few catty comments, made just loud enough for me to hear.

'Oh, how did she get away with that?' 'Who does she think she is?'

'Imagine, falling over like that. How clumsy.' 'She's not a model, she's a circus act.'

But I just tried to ignore them and got on with it.

The most embarrassing time, though, was when I was modelling with Mama in a D&G show. I was wearing a sequined dress and a pair of very high heels, more like stilts . . . I shakily made it halfway down the catwalk, arm in arm with Mama, but then a heel broke and I lost my footing. I fell off the catwalk, taking Mama with me. We landed on top of a couple of shocked photographers who kept clicking as we hit the floor with a big thud.

Mama was horrified but in true professional style faked a smile. The paparazzi had a field day, and the photos landed on the front pages of a couple of magazines and newspapers.

For once Mama and I agreed on something – we were so embarrassed! But Stefano and Domenico loved the extra publicity and insisted on having me appear in their shows. Go figure!

I didn't mind the charity events, since they raised money for many worthy causes. That was the positive side of the business. At least in a roundabout way you could make a difference. But you had to put up with all the trivial gossip about the latest trends and your looks. 'Her legs are fabulous and that hair is divine.' Okay, it could be good for the ego but really, couldn't they chat about something other than looks? I hated the way they talked about me like I wasn't there. I wasn't some plastic mannequin!

# Chapter 3

# The Devils' captains

I wasn't the only one obsessed with football. My papa enjoyed a passion for the round-ball game from the moment he took his first steps. He was thrust into the spotlight early, not only because he was the child of a famous footballer, but because he displayed incredible talent as a youth. He was touted as the next big thing in football from the age of thirteen. And they were right, he was now captain of both AC Milan, known as *Diavoli*, the Devils – one of the world's richest and best football clubs – and the Italian national team. With his beloved Italy, he won the World Cup twice, and he'd won five European Champion trophies with AC Milan.

In the public's eyes Papa was the football legend Paolo Zoffi, but to me he was just Papa. Whenever I got to hang out with him, which wasn't often enough, we'd chill out at home and play with my little chihuahua, Gigi. Papa's always been affectionate, wrapping me up in his huge hugs and telling his silly jokes.

But I didn't get him to myself very often. Papa was so famous that we couldn't walk the streets in our home-town, or in fact anywhere in Italy, without being bothered by the paparazzi or fans. He was very patient with the fans – he'd never say no to a kid asking for an autograph. But it was even worse after a game, when he ventured out to the players' well-known hangouts, such as Giannino's, a restaurant owned by one of his team mates. The photographers would wait in their cars or around the corner and pounce when the players appeared.

Wherever we went as a family it was the same. Very few photographers respected your space; they thought they owned you. The paparazzi even followed us to our retreat in Lake Como sometimes, but at least then they kept their distance. It was so laid-back there. You didn't get any of the noise you were bombarded with in the fastpaced city of Milan. It was gorgeous for a short break but after a while I'd be bored with the peace and quiet, so I always looked forward to returning to the city.

Papa loved Lake Como too, but really, he escaped from it all on the pitch; it was his sanctuary. And he – like the rest of his team – was captivating to watch. Most of all, I loved going to the home games, as the atmosphere at the San Siro stadium was incredible, especially in the local derby where his team faced off against Inter Milan. I usually watched Papa's games from the team's private box. It was luxurious, but I wished I could sit in the grandstand with all the *real* fans more often. Being in the crowd was how I imagined sitting in the Colosseum would have been, watching gladiators fight for their lives in fierce battles against ravenous lions. AC Milan's dedicated fans, known as the *rossoneri* (the red and blacks), would face off with Inter's fanatical supporters, the *nerazzurri* (the black and blues). They'd spur on their teams with loud chanting and wild cheering throughout the spectacle and when their team scored, it was electrifying.

I loved watching Papa and his team mates play – not only were they incredible athletes but really cool guys. If I timed it well, sometimes I got to spend time in the change room before the match, although I had to get out of there when the manager arrived for the team talk. (Well, I actually hid behind a wall so that I could listen to his strategy.) At half-time the talk could become very animated, to put it mildly. Sometimes the manager got angry and exploded with fury. Of course, that was when they were losing. When they were winning, which was quite often, he didn't say much at all.

That was the best thing about being Paolo Zoffi's daughter; I got to break into the inner sanctum. If only he liked the idea that I wanted to follow in his footsteps. Yeah, Papa just didn't get it. He didn't know that I was still playing football. He thought the game was just for boys, and not for his daughter. Girls, he'd say, should be feminine, not sliding into tackles and getting dirty.

We'd see about that!

*

Even before I first saw Papa play in a big match, my love of football was ignited by my dear late Nonno Dino, who was once AC Milan's star goalkeeper and captain, and one of Italy's most respected players. All he knew was football, and when I came along, the first and only grandchild in the Zoffi family, there was initially disappointment because I was the wrong sex. A boy would certainly follow family tradition, but a girl couldn't possibly wear shin pads. Papa was hoping to teach a son the game he'd played all his life, taking him to watch the big matches. When I arrived, he thought he would be the last of the Zoffis to play.

Girls didn't play, especially in the Zoffi family. Zoffi women were expected to be well educated, look glamorous and enjoy the good things in life. I think it was partly because Papa was very protective. But sometimes it was just stifling! Mama would say, 'This game isn't for girls or ladies . . . it's for boys. You should be dancing or playing tennis like the other girls.'

Nonno Dino couldn't help himself, though. As soon as I was born, he took me under his wing and taught me everything he knew about the game.

He spent as much time with me as possible. He even insisted on looking after me when my parents weren't around. So instead of a nanny I had Nonno, plus the help of a chef and housekeeper who lived in the staff quarters. Nonno was like a big kid; we had so much fun together. He was the one who gave me Gigi, when she was just a tiny, skinny little puppy. She'd always been stubborn. Nonno used to say we were just alike.

He also gave me my first football, which made the sound of a bell when it moved. It was my most treasured toy, buried in among all the pink girly stuff in my cot. My earliest memory is of Nonno Dino placing the football at my feet when I could barely walk and showing me how to kick. When I connected with the ball I'd scream with excitement as it jingled along the floor.

He was so excited that I showed interest in kicking the ball that he made sure we'd play every day. By the time I was three, we had progressed to the mini pitch at the back of the estate. Nonno Dino always made it fun. He stuck life-size cartoon characters on the back of the nets. One day it would be a duck called Signor Paperino – also known as Donald Duck – and then Italy's Mickey Mouse, Signor Topolino, and sometimes he'd surprise me with a beautiful white horse. Each day I couldn't wait to run out onto the pitch to see which character I'd face next. I'd try to kick the ball past them as if they were my targets, and when I scored, the duck would tease me. 'Fantaaastic, quack, quack, quack. See if you can beat me again . . . quack, quack.'

I'd be in raptures of laughter until Nonno Dino would throw the ball back out and say, 'Come on, the duck will talk to you again if you can kick the ball past him.'

Nonno was impressed with my ability, even though I was motivated purely by fun. And he loved sharing his treasured tales about my Nonna Lucia, who I was named after. She passed away before I was born. She was the daughter of professors, and broke tradition by forging a successful career as one of Italy's top tennis players. He'd proudly announce that she was the best in Italy, enjoying the top ranking for many years. They were the darlings of Italian sport and the social set.

So even though Papa was old-fashioned about girls playing football, I had a bit of a sporting heritage. It was important to Nonno. 'Lucia,' he used to say, 'you remind me so much of your nonna. You have her natural sporting ability and determination to be the best. Never lose that instinct. Your nonna faced opposition from her parents too but she never gave up and she lived her dream. One day, I know you'll follow the family tradition and be a great player just like your papa. I know you'll prove that girls can also be great footballers. I hope I live to see it.'

I became so obsessed with the game that I used to cuddle up in bed with my football and dream about playing in a big stadium just like my nonno and papa. Some people might have thought that was a bit weird, but I knew there were lots of girls around the world who felt like they didn't fit in. Being a girl didn't always mean you liked playing with dolls and wearing dresses . . . I never did.

Funnily enough, I'd always received them as gifts, and while I learnt to be gracious and accept them, I didn't want them. It would drive Mama crazy.

'I don't understand why you don't play with your dolls and wear those pretty dresses,' she'd say, shaking her head. 'I loved getting such beautiful things when I was your age.'

But to me they weren't beautiful. I had no interest in playing dress-ups and talking to dolls. I'd throw them aside and just play with my ball.

I think Nonno secretly thought this was funny, but he also taught me to be charitable; we would give the unwanted dolls to those in need. He'd come from a very poor background and escaped poverty by becoming a professional footballer. It had been his ticket to a better life, and a better life for his family – but he never forgot how hard his life had once been.

# Chapter 4

# Reality check

I started competing in the local junior football league when I was four, thanks to Nonno Dino. I was the only girl playing, and even back then I had to prove myself. It didn't take long – I quickly gained respect by becoming the top goal-scorer in the league. Everyone took notice of the blonde ponytail heading for the goal.

'Go Lucia, now pass,' Nonno would yell. But I'd just keep running with the ball; it felt too good to stop. I'd weave my way around the defenders and strike the ball as hard as I could, and most of the time I'd find the target.

I was a natural striker, groomed to be selfish by the team coach and the spectators. I believed I was the only goal-scorer – the chosen one. But Nonno wanted me to appreciate being part of a team. He'd give me one *lira* for scoring a goal, but two *lire* for assisting my team mates. He used to say, 'Remember, it's more important to be a team player and have fun playing the game you love than being the star. When the team is happy, so are you.'

But for a long time I didn't listen. He eventually quelled my attitude by teaching me as much as he could about all the positions. He taught me moves and techniques to keep my opponents guessing. 'Stay a step ahead . . . create your chances. Be free with the ball and have fun with it,' he'd say. It was worth it, because my ability to play anywhere made me a sought-after player. Or at least by teams that didn't mind having a ponytail on the pitch.

My parents came to watch a few times, at Nonno's insistence. They only let me play when I was little to appease him, although Papa sometimes got caught up in the action and couldn't help yelling out, 'Go

Lucia. Great goal!' Mama would give him a stern look but he'd just shrug his shoulders.

But those days were over. Now, I had to follow orders and focus on my studies and so-called modelling career. After my parents insisted I quit playing, I had no choice but to leave my club and, worst of all, my team. It felt like I had to start all over again as a footballer. Even getting a game with the kids at my local park was tough. I really had to prove myself. I'd stay until I was given a chance to play, and usually once they saw my ball skills they'd grudgingly let me join in.

Slowly the guys started to accept me – and now I was friends with some of them, especially Pino, who'd become my best friend. I became one of the boys, and they couldn't understand why my parents banned me from playing. They thought it was crazy. But in some ways I wished I was a boy. I overheard my papa say that once, and I kind of agreed it would have made it much easier for me to become a footballer. How stupid! What happened to equal rights?

Sometimes I'd wish I could just fly away and be whoever I wanted to be, and not worry about what anyone thought – other kids, my parents, my teachers. Once I got to the park, that's what it was like. Running with the ball, I'd escape into the pleasure of the game. I'd feel untouchable. Well, until I was brought back down to earth by a fearless defender.

During our training sessions in the park, I usually paired up with Pino, because he was our best defender and we were both fiercely competitive. We'd push each other as much as possible, striving to get the best out of our game. He didn't like it when I beat him, especially in front of the others. The guys would tease him and call him *piccolo* Pino – small Pino. My confidence on the pitch riled him, too. I was always ready with a new trick up my sleeve.

By the end of the game, he'd look at me in disbelief and shout, 'Zeezou, how do you do that?'

One evening, after one of our secret training sessions, I arrived home sweaty, but dressed in my dance outfit with my dirty football gear hidden in my bag. I was so hungry I headed straight for the kitchen, but I stopped in my tracks when I heard a strange snuffling sound. Normally I was the first one home, unless Rosa, our housekeeper, was working late. I cautiously walked into the main living area where the noise was coming from and to my great surprise Mama was curled up on the lounge bawling her eyes out.

She was rarely home before seven o'clock. I stood quietly in the corner of the room, stunned. I wasn't sure what to do or say. We hadn't got on so well since I was forced to quit football, but I couldn't stand seeing her so upset.

I moved closer to comfort her, but as I took the first step, I noticed that my ballet shoes didn't feel right. I looked down and realised I had another problem. If she saw me now, my life wouldn't be worth living.

How could I hide a pair of dirty football boots? I had to get out of here and change, or I could kiss my football dream goodbye. I slowly turned to leave but . . .

'Who's there?' Luckily she didn't look up.

'Hi, Mama, it's me. Are you okay?' I asked hesitantly as I turned back. I was stuck a few metres away from her, hoping desperately that she wouldn't look at me.

'Um, yes thanks,' she mumbled. She took a deep breath and I could see her trying to pull herself together, sniffling and blowing her nose.

I wanted to hug her and find out what was going on but it was too risky.

'Well, if you say so. I'm just going to jump into the shower.' I tried to make a quick, casual exit.

'Lucia, wait . . .' She buried her face in her hands. 'It's about your nanna in Australia. She's been in a car accident and she's in hospital in a serious condition.' Mama started sobbing again.

'Oh no,' I screamed. I was so shocked I just wanted to run away from the horrible news. I fled up to my bathroom, trying to hold back my tears. I couldn't bear the thought of Nanna Betty being in hospital. She'd come to mean a lot to me, especially since Nonno Dino passed away.

Nanna and I spoke on the phone nearly every week, since we hardly ever saw each other face to face. Mama had managed to fly my grandparents over to Italy for surprise visits and to give them a break from their grocery store in Sydney. But I still never saw them often enough. It was more difficult for us to travel to Sydney because Mama didn't like to leave Papa behind, and he couldn't get any time off during the football season. Even in the off-season he had commitments with the club. But he'd been promising that this year he'd find some time off for a trip to Australia. It was just as well. It sounded like my grandparents needed us more than ever.

# Chapter 5

# Sydney

We left for Sydney the next morning on Papa's private jet. He couldn't come with us, as he had to play a fixture that weekend and had other sponsorship commitments he couldn't get out of. So at such short notice, Mama and I had to leave without him – and without poor little Gigi. It was all such a rush, I didn't even get a chance to say goodbye to my friends, not even Pino. I'd just have to call him when we landed. I was going to miss kicking the ball around with him and the boys in the park, but right now Nanna was my priority.

When we arrived, Sydney was wet and miserable . . . yuck. I was expecting it to be sunny and warm but it was grey and dull, reflecting my mood, and the drive from the airport took us through heavy traffic into a bustling modern city. The people walking along the streets were dressed in extremely casual clothes, even thongs. I never saw that in Milan. It'd been so long since I was here that I really didn't remember Sydney at all. I was just a toddler when I was last here with Mama for a brief visit.

We finally got to Nanna and Grandpa's shop in Kings Cross. It was set in a wide, tree-lined street with a mixture of large Victorian terrace houses and modern flats. Grandpa's store was small, yet full of the largest and brightest fruit and vegetables I have ever seen gleaming from the front window. The driver opened the door and in an instant I was swept up in a huge, welcoming hug.

'Lucia, look at you! I'm so happy you came.'

'Dad, how are you?' wept Mama, grasping his hand and reaching for a tissue.

'I'm holding up, and much better now that you're here.' 'How's Mum?'

'She's all right. I can't talk about it now.' A tear slipped down his face.

'Let's have a cup of coffee, then we can go and see her.'

'I'll take our bags upstairs while you two talk,' I said. I needed a little time to myself. It was hard, seeing Grandpa so upset. I walked up into the little apartment above the shop and made myself comfortable on the beige lounge strewn with embroidered flowery red cushions. I was desperate to hear a familiar voice, so I rang Pino. We'd arrived very early in the morning, Sydney time – with any luck he might still be awake.

'Ciao, Pino. It's Zeezou.' 'Ciao. What's up?'

'I'm sorry I didn't have time to let you guys know. I had to come to Sydney.'

'What, Australia? Why?'

'My nanna is in hospital after being hit by a car, so Mama and I had to leave as soon as we could. We're staying with my grandpa. We're going to visit Nanna soon and I'm not looking forward to seeing her hooked up to machines.'

'That's awful, Zeezou. I hope she gets better soon.' 'Me too. Please say hi to the rest of the guys for me.' 'Yeah, of course. How long are you there for?'

'I'm not sure.'

'Oh. Well, we'll miss you down at the park, Zeezou.' 'Ciao, Pino.'

'Ciao.'

We were staying on at my grandparents' place so we could keep Grandpa company and spend more time with him. He didn't seem to be coping very well, so it was a good thing we were there. The place was small, and Mama was already finding it tough having to help out with the housework, which was pretty funny. I'd never seen her domestic side. Watching her wash dishes was hysterical.

'I'm not made for this. I could be more productive with my time. I shouldn't be mopping and cleaning dishes! How do people *do* this every day?' she complained as she wiped down the table one night. The first thing she'd buy here would probably be a dishwasher – the designer shops would have to settle for second place for once. It gave Grandpa a bit of light comic relief to see Mama in an apron. Grandpa told me that even as a kid she used to avoid it . . . she always managed to escape her chores with some excuse.

Two streets away from the shop was the heart of Kings Cross. It was known as an exciting place to party, with lots of nightclubs and trendy restaurants, but it was also deemed an unsafe area. It had a very diverse mix of people. Businesswomen and men in suits frequented the cafés, rubbing shoulders with tourists and labourers. Even celebrities tried to blend in, with Hollywood actors and champion boxers popping in for their caffeine fix.

Mama grew up in the Cross, although she liked to call it Roslyn Gardens. In fact, she grew up right here above the fruit shop. (To my absolute delight, the shop also stocked chocolates and all sorts of treats and other essentials. It was kid heaven, especially since Grandpa had a gelato bar set up at the back of the store.)

Grandpa had been operating the business for over forty-five years. He came to Australia by boat from Lebanon when he was only fifteen years old, without a word of English and only a few shillings in his pocket. That was hard to imagine – I could never be that brave.

Nanna was the next-door neighbours' daughter. Grandpa used to persuade her to sneak off to the park with him. Whenever I spoke to Nanna, she'd tell me some story from their early days, such as how they'd happily stroll along the harbour foreshore, innocently hanging out and talking for hours.

When she was a young girl Nanna dreamt of being an actress, seeing herself on the silver screen and looking glamorous like Marilyn Monroe. She loved the romantic notion of stage and film and her long blonde hair and stunning looks proved a popular mix. Once, when I complained to her about Mama wanting me to model all the time, Nanna had laughed. 'Times change, Lucy! My parents were so dismayed when I started to dabble in the acting world. I was in a few television commercials and TV shows, and performed on stage in theatrical productions, you know.'

'I know, Nanna. Mama's told me she got it from you,' I'd said.

Nanna and Grandpa married at just nineteen years of age and had never been apart since. Two years later, their only child, my mama, was born, and Nanna gave up acting. Mama was named after Frida Kahlo, Nanna's favourite artist. Nanna's been painting since before Mama was born. We had many of her paintings on the walls at home. They were absolutely beautiful – I had a few of them in my bedroom. She used a stunning ruby-red colour in many of her works, and the magical thing about them was that they were so childlike and playful. They always made me feel closer to her.

Mama always encouraged my relationship with Nanna. I think the two of them quarrelled, but loved each other really. That sounded familiar. Talking with Nanna helped me get through a very difficult time after Nonno Dino passed away, and she and Grandpa shared my secret about playing football with Pino and the other guys. She always told me to follow my dreams no matter what my parents have planned for me.

Now I was here for her and that felt good. After all, family came first.

Poor Grandpa. It was killing him seeing his beloved wife fighting for her life. The store was the only thing keeping his mind off the horrible accident that put Nanna in hospital. He loved his fruit shop, meeting people from all walks of life and getting to know the locals. Many of them had become close friends, frequently popping in for a chat and asking after Nanna. He was so engaging and hospitable, it was no surprise that he was so popular with his customers.

Nanna once told me that he'd have Elvis tunes playing in the shop. He'd sing along and swing his hips while serving customers, or grab them for a spontaneous dance in the middle of the store. Nanna said she preferred to look on and admire his zest for life and love of people. She was more of an observer, very private and in her own world, even though she was a different person on stage. When she was hit by a car while crossing the road in front of the shop, Grandpa tried to get a glimpse of the number plate but the driver sped away into the night. Now she was hooked up to a machine in intensive care. She'd already been through three operations; at this point it was still touch and go.

'Lucy, what are you thinking about?' Grandpa gently asked as we walked home from the hospital one evening. Mama and I had been in Sydney for three weeks and visited Nanna every day and most nights. She was still weak, but slowly improving. She was perky enough to tease Mama about her dressy outfit tonight. That was definitely a sign she was on the mend.

'Oh, I want Nanna to be able to walk out of here with us. I just wish that I could help her,' I replied.

'You're helping her by staying with me. I'm so glad that you and your mother are here. I don't know what I'd do without you.'

Grandpa hugged me close as Mama looked over with tears in her eyes.

Poor Mama. She and Nanna had argued over the phone just a few days before the accident, and I suspected Mama was probably feeling guilty about it now. They had been close when Mama was growing up, but when she decided to live in Italy it caused problems in their relationship. Nanna was constantly trying to persuade her to come and live in Sydney, especially after I was born. But Mama was reluctant to give up her glamorous life in Italy. She couldn't come without Papa, either. Grandpa and Nanna visited nearly every year, but they were starting to tire of the long trip, even though Mama had them travelling first class. This time, Nanna was begging Mama to bring me over for an extended holiday and even suggested I continue my schooling in Sydney. But they ended up arguing over the idea and Mama snapped at her.

Mama spent her childhood trying to find a way out of her life in Kings Cross. She wanted something more – she felt she was destined for a more exciting life, and didn't like living above a fruit shop and having to serve customers. When Grandpa spoke Lebanese to her in front of her friends she'd pretend not to understand. She was embarrassed! Back in her day people from different backgrounds were given a hard time and called awful names just because they spoke another language or ate different foods. Thankfully times had changed and we lived in a more tolerant society. Well . . . mostly more tolerant.

I kept thinking that staying here for a while would be good for Mama, and maybe bring her down to earth a little bit. Sydney didn't seem all that bad to me. Over the past few weeks it had grown on me, especially when the sun was out. The city shone and everyone seemed much happier. But it would be even better if I could get a game of football. That thought perked me up.

I gave Grandpa an extra squeeze and then ran ahead. I was desperate to get some exercise after so long sitting in the stuffy hospital room, and I wanted to get away on my own. I bolted down the hill.

'Lucia, you've run past the store,' yelled Mama.

'I'm getting some fresh air. Don't worry Mama, I'll be fine.' I slowed down and half turned around. Mama's mouth opened for a tirade, but I could see Grandpa put his hand on her arm and say something to her.

'Okay then, but be careful,' she called, shrugging. 'Don't stay out too long!'

I'd never ventured down this way before and as I got closer to the bottom of the hill I could hear the most familiar sweet sound of a football being kicked. My heart accelerated to the beat of my run.

And I wasn't disappointed. At the very bottom of the street I found a gate to a park. Just inside was a bench, so I sat down, staring out onto the moonlit pitch. A few guys were getting their last kicks in before the night sky closed in on them.

This was heaven, a perfect pitch just down the road from Grandpa's shop, and with the harbour as the backdrop. It didn't get any better than this. Now I just needed to get my foot on the ball. But I was too late. The guys were picking up their bags and heading off. I stayed on my bench, looking out into the night, wishing for a kick of the ball.

Suddenly I felt a tap on the back of my shoulder. 'Hey, what are you doing here?' came a voice from behind.

'Oh, I was just enjoying the football.' I turned around, slightly startled. Of course, I'd been taught never to talk to strangers but this guy looked harmless. He was around my age and really quite cute, with long shaggy brown hair and big chocolate-brown eyes. I'd just seen him kicking the ball with his friends and he was quite good – but I wasn't going to tell him that.

'A girl that likes football, hey?' said the stranger. 'So, what's it to you?'

'Well, you're hanging around in my territory,' he bit back, 'so I want to know what you're up to.'

'I'm not up to anything, and who says it's your territory, anyway? Who are you?'

'I live here. I'm Roy Spitz. And who are you?'

'I'm a footballer from Italy, where they call me Zeezou.

But off the pitch I'm Lucy Zoffi.'

Roy couldn't stop giggling. 'You're telling me you share a nickname with France's legend, Zinedine Zidane? And I suppose you play like him?' He laughed. 'Next, you'll tell me, Senora Zoffi, that you're related to the great Paolo Zoffi.'

'It's Signorina Zoffi,' I corrected cheekily.

'Oh, so now you're going to teach me Italian.'

'No, I'm going to teach you how to play football. One day I'll be one of the best. Come on, I'll show you.'

'You're confident, but you look like you belong in some silly fashion magazine, not on the football pitch.'

I could feel my face turn red. 'Well, we'll see about that. How about I challenge you to a one-on-one? Then we'll see who the poser is.'

Roy looked a bit shocked, but quickly covered it up. 'Why would I accept a challenge from a girl? Football's not for girls. I don't need to prove myself to you. Go and play dress-ups or whatever you normally do.'

'You sound just like so many other silly boys. Come on, let's play so that I can prove you wrong. I dare you!'

'Go and cry to Daddy. I suppose he's Paolo Zoffi . . . and I'm Zinedine Zidane,' he laughed.

I was tempted to tell him the truth. That would have shut him up, but I didn't want to be known just as Paolo Zoffi's daughter. In fact, this was really my chance to go undercover – to be just me, Lucy. I shouldn't have used my surname. From now on I'd be Lucy Zeezou, on and off the pitch.

'Let's see, are you a footballer or a pretender? Take me on. What are you afraid of?' I taunted.

Next thing I knew he'd shrugged and kicked the ball back onto the pitch. There was just enough light for us to see what we were doing, thanks to the parade of street lights alongside the park and the adjoining tennis courts. 'Game on, Signorina Zoffi. Let's see what you're made of!' he shouted.

We chased the ball, nearly tripping over each other. He got there first and made a run for the goal but I managed to tackle him from the side and win the ball.

He paused momentarily. A look of utter disbelief crossed his face.

'What's up Signor Spitz?' I teased.

'It's getting too dark. I lost sight of the ball but you won't have it for long.' He chased me to the other end of the pitch.

He caught up with me, but not before I took a shot from thirty yards . . . it headed straight for the goal. Roy dived to stop me, catching my ankles and bringing me down, but it was too late.

'Referee, did you see that? An illegal tackle . . . a red card!' I yelled.

Out of nowhere a little dog ran onto the pitch and stopped the ball centimetres from the goal line.

'No, that was about to be a goal!' I bellowed.

We broke into laughter as the cute dog played with the ball. He reminded me of Gigi – he had the same funny run. I missed my little treasure.

I jumped to my feet and made a run for the ball. The dog had managed to dribble it back to the halfway line. I chased it down like my life depended on it and regained possession. The dog wasn't happy and gave chase, biting at my feet, but I managed to keep the ball, although I was giggling so hard I was barely in control.

I kicked the ball up into the air and volleyed it into the back of the net. Whoosh! Oh, that felt so good.

I celebrated in typical goal-scoring fashion without thinking. I lifted my top up and ran around the pitch as if I'd just won the World Cup. Of course the boys at home were used to my antics, but I'd kind of got swept up in the moment.

Just then I could hear Mama yelling, 'Lucia? Lucia, where are you?'

I came to a very quick halt – I couldn't let her see me on the pitch. I pulled down my top. Thankfully I had my singlet on underneath.

'I'm coming, Mama, I'm coming.' I turned to Roy and said, 'Um . . . I've got to go. Ciao, Signor Spitz.'

'That was a lucky goal, Signorina Zoffi. Ciao!' He looked stunned.

'Maybe next time the ball will roll your way, if you're lucky like me. See ya!'

'Yeah, Zeezou . . . see you at the next session.' He gave me a little smirk and walked off.

Wow – the next session? Cool. I didn't know what to say, but then Mama appeared. I sprinted up to her with a smile etched across my face and a tingling tummy.

'Lucia, what were you doing?' Mama asked.

I looked around, but luckily Roy wasn't anywhere to be seen. 'I was just exploring the neighbourhood,' I replied innocently. 'And Mama, can you please call me Lucy?'

'What's this Lucy business? Your name is Lucia and you should be proud of it.' Mama put her hands on her hips dramatically.

'Yes, but in Australia the translation is Lucy and that's what I want to be called. I just want to fit in. It's hard enough being Paolo Zoffi's daughter. I want my own identity and my own life. So please, Mama, just call me Lucy,' I stressed.

'Lucia, you silly thing. How can Paolo Zoffi's daughter blend in? You should be proud to be a Zoffi and proud to be Italian. And you know you're named after your father's late mother. Lucia is a beautiful name and very sophisticated.' She sounded quite huffy now.

'I know that. I'm proud *of* all those things but I want my own identity. I want you to call me Lucy. Why is it so hard for you to support me?' I howled.

Parents just had to take control. I always had to fight for what I truly wanted. I wasn't giving up. I'd give anything to get back onto that pristine pitch with Roy and fight for the ball. At least there I could be Lucy Zeezou and nobody else – just me. Even Roy called me Zeezou! I wondered when I'd see him again.

# Chapter 6

# Oranges and apples

'Hey, Lucy, would you mind helping me out a little bit in the shop today?' Grandpa asked. 'I could do with an extra hand.'

'I'd love to but I was just about to –'

'My helpers are always given extra servings of gelato,' he added.

'Now you're talking. Sure, Grandpa, I'm all yours.'

I started working, stacking the shelves with big, colourful oranges, shiny apples, mandarins and mangoes. The smell of the fresh fruit made me hungry.

I'd taken a big bite on a juicy apple when my first customer walked in, a scruffy-looking boy around my age in a school uniform.

'Hi, can I help you?' I asked.

'Yep. Just the chips and drink, thanks,' he replied, smiling at me.

'Hi, Harry,' Grandpa called out.

'Oh! Hi, Mr Dib. How's Mrs Dib getting along?' 'She's getting better every day, thanks. How are the Lions going?' Grandpa asked.

That pricked up my interest in my customer. The Lions? Sounded like a football team. Probably one of those dodgy Australian codes of football, I told myself. But just then I glanced down at Harry's bag, sitting on the ground. Guess what was peeping out of it?

Now I was jumping out of my skin. This was my big chance to get a kick around and maybe even find a team. 'We're doing really well, sitting at second spot on the league table. But we've just lost Gadi, our top goal-scorer. He tore his hamstring after a massive tackle last weekend.

He'll probably be out for the rest of the season.' Harry made a face.

'That's no good. Don't you have someone to replace him?'

'Nah, we're trialling for a new striker on Friday after school. If you know anyone who can score lots of goals, please tell them to come to the Reg at four o'clock. But they've gotta be fourteen, turning fifteen next year to qualify for our age group.' Harry picked up his bag and put it over his shoulder.

No – don't go! This was my big chance. The right age group and everything. I would have loved to trial but he was probably looking for a guy. So what, I had to try. I had to think of something before he left.

'Um, maybe I can help you,' I bumbled, without knowing what I was going to say next.

'Oh, silly me, I haven't introduced you. Harry this is my granddaughter, Lucy. She's over here from Italy with her mum, helping me out while Mrs Dib recovers.'

'Hi, Lucy. You're lucky to have such nice grandparents. You reckon you can help me find a striker? Who do you have in mind?'

Think quickly, Lucy. I couldn't tell him it was me. I was always putting my foot in it. 'Um, a friend of mine called L . . . Lucas,' I lied.

'Is he a local?'

'Well, kind of. I think he lives around here,' I said tentatively. Keep it together, Lucy.

'Funny, I don't know a Lucas and I've lived here all my life. Anyway it doesn't matter, we're desperate. Bring him down to the Reg on Friday for a trial and we'll see how he goes. If he makes it, he'll need a photo and a guardian to sign the registration form.'

'Yes, I'm . . . um . . . he's the right age and I'm sure he can sort out the rest,' I stumbled.

I was desperate to join a team and play competitively again. At least here, away from the usual scrutiny, I was more likely to get away with it. I was so excited I could hardly contain myself. But now I was in a little bit of a pickle. I'd have to involve Grandpa . . . there was no other way.

'Harry, I expect you to look after my one and only granddaughter. She's very precious to me,' Grandpa said, smiling.

Grandpa was being sweet, but how embarrassing! I didn't need to be looked after; I could take care of myself. This guy would think I was a prissy, helpless girl. I wondered if they had any girls in his team. I couldn't ask in case it raised suspicion.

'Ah, sure, Mr Dib, no worries. But she might get a bit bored, since we mostly play football and we don't play with girls. But Lucy can hang out with us as long as she doesn't mind watching a game.' Harry looked over at me quizzically.

Well, that answered my question. Lucas it was.

Now my time in Sydney was looking up – a football pitch down the road from the shop and a new friend who shared my passion for the game. I had to play it cool.

'Oh, that's okay, Harry. It'll be nice to just hang out. I'll see you Friday.' I tried to sound casual.

'Yeah, great! I can't wait to meet Lucas and check out his moves.'

'I'm sure you'll like him. I'm, I mean, he's a natural up front. I've got a feeling he's just what you're looking for.'

'Cool, see you Friday then. Bye, Mr Dib.' Harry made his way out.

Grandpa looked at me. 'Great to see you're making friends, Lucy. I'm so proud of you.'

'Thanks Grandpa, but please don't tell Mama that I'm going to hang out with footballers. She'll go nuts. Please, please don't tell her.'

He put his arm around my shoulder. 'I know your dilemma, but I still think it's crazy that you have to secretly play the game that's your dad's profession. Football is a big part of your life. And besides, there's no harm in you spending time with Harry. He's a good kid.'

I rolled my eyes. 'You don't understand. She doesn't even want me hanging out with footballers! We really have to keep it quiet. But when I make the team will you please sign my form for me?'

His jaw dropped. '*Oh*. Of course, I'll take care of the registration but what about Lucas? How on earth are you going to pull it off? Surely they'll recognise that you aren't one of them.' He laughed.

'Don't worry, Grandpa, I have it all figured out.'

He gave me a cuddle. 'I'm sure you have, princess. Life is much more fun with you around. You have my full support and your secret is safe with me. Anything for my Lucy.'

'Lucia, where are you?' yelled Mama.

'*Luuucy* is in the shop with Grandpa. Mama, can you please remember that it's Lucy?'

She came running down the stairs like a tornado. 'Nanna's doctor says she's out of danger but it's going to take her a long while to get back on her feet and regain her strength. She's going to need a lot of help.' She put her arms around me.

'That's great, I can't wait to see her home.'

'Well, we'll be seeing a lot more of her, honey, because we're going to stay here for an extended period to help. I've spoken at length to Papa about this and he agrees. Unfortunately he won't be able to join us for a while because of his football commitments. But don't worry, we'll go over soon to spend some time with him and collect Gigi and some of our things.'

Hang on – *collect Gigi*? I was in shock. 'Mama, what do you mean? How long do you think we're going to stay for? I miss Papa and Gigi and my friends, I want to be with them. Italy's our home.' I was on the verge of crying.

I was so confused. Yesterday, I felt on top of the world. I made my first friend in Australia, someone who also happened to be into football. I was even closer to my grandparents and just starting to feel good about this place. But staying here indefinitely – that's something I wasn't expecting.

I was certain about one thing: I was trialling for that football team this Friday and I was going to make sure they selected me. No matter what it took.

'Since we're going to be staying here for a little while longer, you're going to attend school here,' Mama continued. 'You've already missed half this term, but it'll be a good experience for you to go to school in Sydney for a little while. I've enrolled you in a school that's only fifteen minutes up the road. Your papa's club president recommended the school through a good friend whose daughter Bella is a student there. We'll meet her on Monday when you start.'

'Okay, fine Mama.' Monday!

'And there's a studio in the church hall at the top of this street that has dance classes you could go to.'

'Great, I can't wait.' What else could I say? Mama was right. We had to stay and help out, but we also needed to get on with our lives. And for now it looked as though our lives were going to be here. I was a little nervous at the thought of such a big change, but a little excited at the same time.

I excused myself. I needed to call Pino. He'd help me make sense of this.

'Ciao Pino, it's Zeezou.' 'Hey, how are you?'

'I'm okay but I just found out that I'm staying in Australia indefinitely. I have to start school here on Monday.'

'What? That's crazy.'

'I know. I'm confused. On one hand I want to stay to be with my grandparents but on the other . . . I'm going to miss my friends and Milano. Mama says that we're needed here, and I guess she's sacrificing her dream life for a while too. I respect her for that; it's a very big move, especially for her. But I do have some exciting news.'

'More news! What could be bigger than that?'

'I'm trialling for a team here. It's towards the end of their season but it's better than no football. And no one here knows who I am, so I can play competitively. The only thing is that I have to pretend to be a boy to get on the team.'

'What? Are you nuts? You're too, um, well, you know, too, um, girly-looking.'

'Me? Oh Pino, I'm just like one of the boys – they'll never guess.

Anyway don't worry, it'll work out.'

'I hope you know what you're doing. It sounds like a mess! Anyway you can't just stay there. You're Milanese through and through. How will you cope? How about your papa? What does he think?'

'Papa thinks we should stay and help until Nanna is back on her feet, at least for the next few months. What else can I do?'

'Well, I suppose he's right but well . . . we'll miss you, Zeezou.'

'I'll miss you guys too.'

'I'd better go. Call again soon, okay?' 'Okay. Speak soon. Ciao.'

# Chapter 7
# Secret identity

Over the next few days I was too full of excitement at the prospect of trialling for a team to think much about leaving Milan behind. The timing was perfect. Now that I knew I'd be here for at least a few more months, I could make more of a commitment and it'd make life much more bearable. And the best thing was that Lucy Zeezou was unknown. I could be myself, not Lucia Zoffi, with all that went with that name.

Things were feeling much more settled. Mama had organised a driver for us, and someone to help around the house. She was spending more time with old friends from her modelling days, heading off to lunches and functions. And by Friday, even Grandpa seemed much more cheery.

'Mama, I'm off to dance class,' I said breezily.

'Okay, but come home straight afterwards, we're off to see Nanna after Grandpa closes up.'

Mama was busy getting dolled up to head out. She really was starting to enjoy Sydney.

'Don't worry, Mama, I'm not far away. Anyway, you're out for the day,' I beamed.

'I'll be back early. I'm just off for a quiet lunch with a few old friends.' She shrugged and continued to apply her make-up.

Amazing. Ever since Mama's big speech about staying here indefinitely, she'd loosened the reins. I was making the most of my freedom before the clamps came down again. I guess she was still worried about Nanna. Or maybe it was just that here in Sydney, without the pressure of the media and the paparazzi, without the pressure of being Zoffis, she felt much more relaxed. In Italy we'd even received a few threats against our family. The police thought it could be a prank from obsessed rival football fans, but there was also a chance it was something worse, such as an organised crime outfit. Who knew what the truth was, but the threats had impinged on my life, as Mama became even more protective of our safety. Thankfully, she was at ease here.

I left the house in my dance outfit with my football gear hidden in my bag and a hat to disguise my hair.

The dance classes were held just up the street so I could walk to football without raising suspicion. All I had to do was stroll up the hill to the church hall, go round the block and sneak back downhill, and I'd be at the heavenly football pitch known as the Reg.

I arrived at the grounds early and ran into the ladies' toilets to transform into Lucas. I tied my long hair into a tight bun and pinned on a short, blond wig I'd borrowed from Nanna's collection of old theatre costumes. Then I secured a cap with bobby pins. I was a tomboy anyway, so I didn't have to worry about my walk. Being tall also helped, and my body was very slim – boy-like in fact – but of course my face could have been a bit of a give-away. I had to remember to keep the cap's brim low.

As I walked out towards the pitch, some of the players were already warming up. I caught sight of Harry at the entrance. I started running in his direction, forgetting myself as the thought of playing with my new football friend took over. Then I came to a sudden halt.

What was I doing?

Harry was expecting to see Lucy *and* Lucas. Oh no. If I'd been a boy, life in the football world would be much easier, but I was happy being a girl. I just wished that we were treated equally. Well, today I was a boy . . . and hopefully a convincing one. I mustered all of my courage, walked up to Harry and introduced myself with my deepest voice.

'Hi, Harry, I'm Lucas,' I mumbled from under my hat. 'Hey, Lucas. How did you know my name?' Harry asked, inspecting me very closely.

I lowered my gaze. 'Lucy gave me a very good description.' I hoped I sounded at least halfway convincing.

'Where is Lucy?' Harry looked around quizzically.

'Oh, she can't make it. She asked me to apologise but she had to visit her nanna in hospital. She'll see you another time.'

'I hope so . . . I mean, uh . . . I hope her nanna's okay. Lucy seems like a nice girl and she's, uh, quite pretty, don't you think?' Harry looked at the ground.

Then I was really struggling. Blood rushed through my face and I could tell I was doing my best beetroot impression – not a good look. I might have been used to photographers telling me that I looked good, but that was part of their job. This was the first time a boy my own age had been this complimentary to my face – although, technically, he wasn't really telling me was he? I started to walk out onto the pitch, then nonchalantly replied, 'Yeah, she's okay.'

'Uh, wait, how do you know Lucy?' Harry asked.

Still red-faced, I replied, 'We've been good friends for a long time. We used to play football together when we were little in Italy. Anyway, let's play.' I shook my head. That was a dumb thing to say – I should have come up with something better.

'You played in the same team as Lucy?' Harry sounded incredulous. 'I didn't know she could play football. I reckon girls should play against each other and leave the boys to it. They're not tough enough to play with or against boys and they're too slow. Anyway, come over and meet Coach James. He's a funny Irishman who *loves* his football.'

So. It was a good thing I was trialling as a boy or I would never have got this opportunity. Now I was even more determined to get into this team – and I was going to score so many goals they wouldn't hesitate in selecting me.

Harry would freak when he eventually found out the truth but right now I didn't care. Why did boys think they were so much better? Some extremely talented and tough female players have made their names on the world stage, such as the legendary Mia Hamm and Brandi Chastain from the US, Italy's Carolina Morace and top goal-scorer Elizabetta Vignotto, Australia's Lisa De Vanna and Cheryl Salisbury and Brazil's Sissi, and Marta, who is revered in her home nation alongside male stars like Ronaldinho and the great Pele. I couldn't wait for the day my name was mentioned among such amazing players.

It was unbelievable; finally, after four long weeks, I was on the pitch, about to get my first real touch of the ball . . . while impersonating a boy. It didn't get much crazier. Although how was I going to reveal my true identity? I couldn't be Lucas forever.

I was put up front with Harry. I wasn't in the mood to play alongside him but willed myself to think of the bigger picture. I'd deal with him later.

'Hey, Lucas, over here,' Harry yelled.

He was in space on the other side of the pitch. I sent the ball flying over to him and it landed perfectly, at his feet. He charged his way through a few defenders, making his way towards the goal. He was up against the sweeper; the midfielder was calling for it, as he was free, but instead Harry shimmied past and then unloaded.

I pounced on the ball and struck it with all my might – it sailed past the keeper with ease – bang. My first goal.

I was so excited I jumped up and down in ecstasy. Harry ran over to congratulate me. 'Good goal. Let's see you bag another one.'

'Thanks!'

I couldn't have dreamt of a better start – but this was going to be tougher than I'd thought; the standard of the other players was very good. I was just going to have to let my feet do the talking. I decided to work on my defending to show the coach that I was a versatile player. I didn't know who else they'd trialled or what I might be up against.

Now the other players were a little warier of me and tried to keep me out of the play.

Down the other end, a guy named Max was about to shoot from outside the box. I sprinted towards him, slid in and took the ball from under his legs. He fell, crying foul play but it wasn't – it was a fair tackle. Although play continued, Max, who seemed to be one of the key members of the team, was furious.

He brought the game to a standstill, bellowing at the top of his lungs, 'Hey, you with the hat, what the hell do you think you're doing?'

'I was just doing my job. It was a fair tackle,' I replied confidently.

'No, it wasn't,' he yelled. 'You came in from behind and brought me down. That's a foul in my book.'

'Well, the rest of us saw it differently,' I insisted, even though nobody else had come to my defence.

'I don't know who you think you are. Anyway, what kind of footballer wears a hat on the pitch? It's weird and so is your voice!'

'Hey, that's enough,' Harry interrupted. 'Leave Lucas alone and let's get on with it.'

'Well what's he doing defending when he should be up front? That was a foul. Didn't you see it?' Max snapped.

Coach James yelled from the sideline. 'Come on guys, keep playing. You're wasting time. Let's give the new players a fair chance to prove themselves. Max, I need you to focus in your role as left back . . . there's no need for you to be shooting.'

Now I really had to perform some magic. That Max guy was already suspicious. But there was something fishy about him, too; he seemed familiar to me but I couldn't place him. But there was no time to worry about that now. I had to stay focused on winning a spot on the team.

Over the next half-hour the competition on the pitch intensified as the boys started playing more aggressively, but I was up to the challenge. Max, in particular was heavily marking me – giving me a really hard time.

Harry made a break down the right-hand side and sent a spectacular cross in. I made my run among a swarm of defenders, with Max breathing down my neck, desperate to reach the ball first. The 18-yard box was a battleground; there was nudging, elbowing and fierce fighting for position as we all hustled for the ball.

The only way I could win the contest was to come up with the unexpected. Nonno Dino always taught me to act instinctively, moving like a panther ready to pounce on its prey.

Somehow I managed to break free from the pack, and with my back to the goal I leapt into the air and scissor-kicked the ball towards the goal. It catapulted past my rivals.

Some of the boys started clapping as I landed on my backside with a big thud. I wasn't sure if they were celebrating a goal or my fall. I looked up to see the ball nestled in the back corner of the net. I broke into a satisfied smile, thrilled that I'd secured my second goal, and surely a spot on the team.

But instead of congratulations, an eerie silence filtered through the air.

I could see Harry and Coach James running towards me while the rest of the players crowded around. Everyone was staring at me!

They must have been impressed. Had they never seen a scissor kick before?

But by the look on Harry's face, I could tell that something was wrong . . . seriously wrong. I couldn't work it out until the guys started pointing at me, sniggering.

I slowly moved my hands towards my head and my worst fear was realised. I could feel my hair, long and free. No hat and no wig. They must have fallen off when I jumped into the air to glide the ball in for the best goal I'd scored in ages. It had felt so good, but that moment was quickly slipping away.

'I knew something wasn't right about you.' Max looked startled and angry at the same time.

'Look, I can explain,' I pleaded as I looked into Max's eyes – and then it dawned on me.

He'd had a hair cut, that was why I hadn't recognised him – but his name wasn't Max. He was the guy I'd had a kick around with recently.

But I didn't have time to question him or defend myself. Harry jumped in angrily, picking up the hat and wig and shaking them in disbelief. 'Explain what? The fact that you lied?' he yelled. 'Lucas wasn't . . . isn't . . . you're really Lucy from Italy who just *happens* to play football. Why didn't you tell me?'

'Harry, I'm so sorry. I wanted to but I couldn't,' I explained frantically. 'You said that girls don't belong on the pitch. I thought this was my only chance.'

'You should have told us the truth but instead you chose to embarrass me and the rest of the guys.'

Then Max added to the confusion.

'Zeezou? I can't believe it. I should have known . . .' Max and Harry looked at each other.

Max had finally realised that I was the girl he'd met at the Reg. So why had he told me his name was Roy? Now I was confused, and before I could get an answer out of him, Coach James intervened.

'Okay, boys and Lucas – or is it Lucy? I think we need a break after that entertaining encounter. I've never seen anything like this in all of my footballing life . . . a memorable moment indeed!'

I wasn't sure if Coach James was making fun of the situation or if he really meant it. All I knew was that I didn't want to face anyone . . . I just sat there with my head down, wishing this was a nightmare and I was about to wake up and start a new day.

My stomach was churning and the pain in my backside had subsided as a numb feeling set in. I thought of the consequences of my actions and it wasn't a very good forecast. I'd ruined my chances of making the team and maybe any team in Sydney – all in under an hour of playing the game I loved.

I had to hold back my tears to look tough in front of them. Coach James must have sensed that I was close to losing it. He knelt down and did his best to comfort me, with a gentle tone and his hand on my shoulder. 'Lucy-Lucas, what you did was dishonest. I don't know why you thought you had to lie to get a game but I must admit that it was funny. Boy or girl, you've really got talent. That goal was sensational . . . we'll call it the Lucy snap.'

We started laughing and I began to feel better.

'There you go, a smile makes all the difference,' he said kindly. 'I don't know what it's like in Italy, but in Australia football's the number one sport for girls, even though there are some boys still getting used to the idea that girls can play. I coached a women's team back in Ireland and they can really play. Football is for everyone, that's the beauty of the game.' He helped me up and we headed off the pitch to join the others.

I took a deep breath. 'I didn't know what to expect and I was so desperate to play that I was willing to try anything to get into the team. I thought I had a better chance as a boy because I guessed that female footballers weren't accepted.' My voice started to wobble. I was on the verge of tears. 'I'm so sorry, I didn't want to lie and believe me, I didn't like being Lucas anyway. But it doesn't matter now, because I've blown it.'

We all sat down on the sideline, while Coach James stood in front of us to address the players.

'First of all Lucy-Lucas, I think you're an extremely talented player and you definitely proved how much you love this game. Talent, passion and commitment are what I look for in my players and you have those qualities in abundance. And most importantly, I look for creativity, and you certainly have that. Boys, I hope you'll support Lucy as she's one of us – a footballer and a very good one.' 'Oh, come on Coach, she's not that good,' Harry interjected. 'We need a real striker for tomorrow's game, not some long blonde spaghetti from Italy.'

'Harry, I don't like your attitude. We're an inclusive team and that means boys and girls from all backgrounds are welcome to play. That's what football is all about. It was a misunderstanding and it was funny.'

A few of the boys sniggered. Coach James went on. 'I think that we can appreciate Lucy's uncanny efforts. She took extreme measures to play the game we all love, and she's proved that she's an enormous talent.' A few of the boys nodded. 'You're kidding. You can't let a girl play in our team.

And she lied to all of us. If she's in, I'm out of here.' Max stood up and walked off.

I almost expected the rest of them to join him but, surprisingly, nobody else moved. 'If Lucy's good enough to score goals like that, she's good enough to play in our team,' one of the boys said.

'That's right, Dylan,' Coach James agreed. 'I've made my decision. Lucy's on the team and that's final. Lucy, welcome to the 14 A's Dunbar Lions football team . . . you're our first lioness.'

# Chapter 8

# Impostor

I was dressed in the pale pink and blue Dunbar Lions football kit, bolting down a deserted pitch to score a goal. Then my team mate Harry appeared, standing stock-still on the goal line. As I made my way to the edge of the box, about to shoot, he thrust forward a big red STOP sign.

I paused, and then another sign appeared. WRONG WAY, GO BACK.

He had to be kidding . . . what was he doing? No one was stopping me, so I manoeuvred around him and unleashed the ball with all my might. It soared into the top left-hand corner of the goal.

Harry was furious. He walked over to the ball, picked it up and took it to the edge of the eighteen-yard box, and sat on it.

He then held up another sign, this time a pink one. NO GIRLS ALLOWED.

How dare he! I was so furious I kicked the ball from under him and scored another goal as he fell on his bottom.

Next thing I knew I was in my tutu, dancing around the pitch to the sounds of Swan Lake, one of Mama's favourite pieces.

Once I finished my performance I took a bow. When I looked up I could see that Max had joined Harry. They stood together with their arms folded. Gradually they raised their arms to reveal *IMPOSTOR* scrawled in blood-red on their forearms.

I woke up in a sweat.

*Impostor.* I wasn't an impostor . . . I was a footballer and a girl. Why was it so hard to believe?

I pulled myself out of my dreamlike state to face the reality that I was running late for my first game with the Dunbar Lions. Oh, no, they'd be warming up . . . and if I didn't get there right now I'd be stuck on the bench.

I frantically reached for my dance gear. I hesitated – it's not usual to wear a tutu to classes, but wearing it might make Mama think I was really taking dancing seriously. I slipped it on and packed my football kit into my bag. I was going to look so silly walking down the street like this, but I didn't care.

I ran down the stairs, yelling, 'Off to dance class . . . running late, see you soon. Bye.'

Grandpa gave me a wink and a quick 'Good luck', and I was on my way.

I sprinted straight down to the Reg – there was no time to take my usual route around the block. As I'd suspected, they were in the middle of the warm-up, so I joined the back of the line as Coach James took them through their paces.

'Looking sharp, Dylan . . .'

'Come up, Morgan, wee volleys . . . excellent!' 'Dugald, first touch, then pass . . . Touch and pass . . .' 'That's what it's all about today guys. On your toes . . . touch and play it!'

'Ah, Lucy? Did we not give you a strip?

The boys stopped in their tracks. Coach James was giving me an awfully odd look.

'Lucy, you know how to make an entrance. I don't know if this is part of your Italian sense of humour but you cannot be serious. We're here to play football, not perform the *Nutcracker*.'

'Sorry, Coach James, um . . . I've just been to my dance class, that's why I'm running late. I didn't want to miss any more of the warm-up so I thought I'd just join in and change later.'

The boys were laughing, enjoying my humiliation.

Coach James tried to settle the players.

'Okay, that's enough. We've all been late before. We must focus on the game . . . it's a big one.'

Harry, laughing along with the others, couldn't help himself, 'Oh, but Coach James, this must be the first time in the history of the game that a footballer has turned up on the pitch dressed like that.'

'Right, Harry, one more word and you'll be keeping the bench warm for most of the game – and that goes for the rest of you, too. And Lucy, you know the rules. Those who are late, don't start.'

I was furious with myself, but I knew I had to keep it together and hope that I got a run to prove myself.

Coach James continued. 'Boys and twinkle toes, this is an important game against Queens Park. They're currently sitting on top of the table, but not for long. We need a victory today for a crack at winning the league. The team I'll send out are those who have impressed me at training and have been committed to the sessions. I want to be clear . . . I don't like leaving anyone out but it's very competitive with a squad of sixteen and just eleven spots to fill, so those of you who aren't starting will just have to be patient.'

I tuned out in frustration. I hated being stuck on the bench. So close, yet so far . . . I had to be one of the patient ones, in my first competitive game in a year.

I zoned back in on Coach James's team talk. 'Morgan told me last week that he hated me because he didn't start. I was very upset.' He made a face and pretended to cry. Everyone laughed. At least this coach had a good sense of humour. He made things fun, so you wanted to play your best for him and the team. 'Anyone not getting a full game, please don't hold it against me,' he continued. 'I'm trying to be fair. This is the line-up: Felix in goal, and Callum, I want you starting on the left, up front with Harry on the right. Dylan and Morgan in the centre, Jared on the left wing and Dugald on the right. Brandan, Jonathon, Jasper and Taj are our back four. The rest of you will get a game. Heads up, we're all in this together.'

I got the impression it was an unusual line-up, as the team was looking at each other in disbelief. There was also a key player missing. It looked like Max had kept to his word and quit the team.

Coach James kept a cool demeanour. 'We're at the business end of the season and we must play with the right intensity. Up front, I want plenty of movement. Midfield, it's important we support our strikers. Defenders,

I want a clean sheet today. Enjoy yourselves out there, play good attacking football and we'll win. Lucy, I think it's time for you to change into your Dunbar kit. No more, um, tutus. They're out this season.' He smiled.

I ran into the toilet to change and emerged dressed in the team strip, eager to get a run.

'That's better Lucy, now you're one of us. Right, Dunbar Lions?'

'Yes, Coach James,' they echoed croakily, except for Harry, who was fiddling with his boots.

'We must focus. I want to see you work as a unit. Keep it nice and tight, compact. This is all about desire: the team who wants it most will win. We're undefeated at home so let's keep up our winning record. Let's go Dunbar.'

The team spirit lifted as we leapt into the air to give each other high fives. A couple of the guys connected with me, but not Harry. Clearly he was still mad. The boys made their way onto the pitch led by our captain, Brandan. Jared came over and gave me a pat on the back before he headed out. It was good to get that support just before the kick-off.

We started our attack from the outset, making good ground with a couple of one-twos. Just ten minutes into the game, a defender came in with a crunching tackle on Callum, who was making a run down the left-hand side. He crumbled to the ground, clutching his right ankle.

Coach James called me up. 'Lucy, start warming up in case he has to come off.'

He ran on to check Callum's condition and it didn't look good. He couldn't put weight on his right leg. He grimaced with pain.

Coach James alerted the referee he was making a change. 'Lucy, on you go. I want to see some goals from you.'

I took a few deep breaths to settle my nerves and ran onto the field. The opposition glared in disbelief as I took my position. To my surprise, I also heard some encouraging words from the sidelines.

'Go girl.'

'Come on, lioness.'

Some of our rivals weren't as welcoming. 'Ponytail, you're in the wrong game!'

'Who's the girly?'

The comments didn't bother me – I'd heard them all before. Besides, there was too much to be done on the pitch to think about that. Queens Park proved to be a very tough opponent. I had to get stuck in and perform at my best if I was going to make an impression.

Despite playing with the home advantage, it was Queens Park who dominated the first half, but our keeper, Felix, managed to keep a clean sheet with some spectacular saves.

The boys were hesitant to pass the ball to me – especially Harry – and ignored my pleas when I was in space. Now I could hear the coach yelling, 'Pass it to Lucy, she's free. Lucy's free!', but Harry ignored him and went it alone. His shot was blocked by a sea of defenders. I was left standing alone, dejected and shocked that he was so angry with me that he'd jeopardise the game. We could have been leading 1–0.

'Come on Dunbar, lift your game. Mark up!' yelled Coach James.

Against the run of play, Queens Park worked the ball through the midfield. Their engine room masterfully combined to find their playmaker, who bypassed two defenders and found their striker up front, poised to attack. He outmanoeuvred our sweeper and sent the ball into the back of the net to give Queens Park a 1–0 lead.

They celebrated in style, the goal-scorer Zakk expressing his delight with a cartwheel and an impressive flip. Their fans chanted and cheered as the half-time whistle blew.

We walked over to Coach James with our heads down. We'd played so hard and expected to be in the lead, but instead we were trailing at the break . . . it was disheartening.

The parents ran over with drinks for their kids, but of course I had to get my own. Mama thought I was at my dance class, working on my pirouettes. I wouldn't want her here anyway: she'd have turned up with perfect hair and make-up, head to toe in dressy designer gear and high heels . . . she had no idea. I certainly didn't need any more stick, especially now.

Coach James called us in for his half-time talk. 'In you come. On one knee.' He saw me give him a strange look. 'Staying upright instead of slumping on the ground will keep you alert. Now, this is the worst I've seen you play all season. Too many back heels and flicks. No need to be fancy. There's not enough urgency in what we're doing. Dugald, we need you back in defence, swap positions with Brandan. Dylan, you've been the best player in the first half. Keep up the good work. Morgan, as usual you've been working tirelessly. Keep running at them. Jasper, if Dylan or Morgan goes, sit back into midfield. Brandan, when you get the ball, relax and enjoy it. Take your time . . . put your foot on the ball and do it simply. Boys, one other thing. Lucy is giving you options and you're not utilising her when she's in space. She's being ignored.'

Brandan spoke up. 'Coach, I think we're just not used to playing alongside a girl. No offence, Lucy, we're not sure how to include you.'

Coach James responded, 'Brandan, thanks for your honesty. Lucy is one of us. If it helps, call her "Zeezou", it's her nickname. Is that okay, Lucy?'

'Of course, I'd love that,' I replied.

'You must look out for her and pass her the ball. It's really disappointing that you're not including her, but now I understand it's not intentional. So, if Zeezou calls for the ball, look up and pass it to her. It's a team effort that will help us win the game. So let's do it, Dunbar.'

As the rest of the players ran back on to the pitch, Coach James took me aside and encouraged me to roam in midfield and run with the ball to set up Harry. He also had a private word with Harry, and whatever was said, Harry ended up with a smile on his face. Coach James seemed to know how to get the best out of his players. Pino would really like him.

We ran back on for the second half, a goal down. Harry still hadn't spoken to me, but I was feeling much more relaxed on the pitch and determined to make an impact.

We came out firing. Dylan, our talented midfielder, wove his magic in the middle of the pitch and kicked a beautiful through ball for me to chase. I just had to beat the sweeper.

'Good ball, Dylan . . . now back her up. Go, Zeezou, win it!' Coach James yelled.

I ran with such utter desperation that I tripped over my feet . . . the crowd roared. I bounced straight back up but I was too late. My opponent had the ball and tried to work his way back up the pitch.

I managed to win the ball back and pressed on as my team mates made their way into the box. I crossed the ball, hoping to find Harry, who was lurking among the defenders. He leapt higher than the rest, heading the ball straight past the besieged keeper to level.

Cheers echoed from the sidelines and Coach James was the proudest of all. 'Great work Dunbar. Well done Harry . . . that's it, Zeezou, let's keep it up Lions.'

Harry was mobbed by the rest of the team, celebrating his magnificent goal. I stood alone, wondering what else I had to do to become a part of this team, when to my surprise a few of the boys ran over to me.

'Superb cross, Zeezou,' offered Dylan. Jasper and Dugald gave me a high five.

Brandan, the captain, gave me a big smile. 'Great job, Zeezou. Keep it up.'

And then the one that counted most. 'Hey, Lucy Zeezou, thanks. Perfect cross,' said Harry.

'That was a brilliant header, very impressive,' I replied.

He gave me a high five and a smile.

I think that was the start of our friendship. Whatever Coach James said to him must have sunk in. I'd earned respect as a team player and that's what it was all about. I understood exactly what Nonno Dino had meant about a happy team.

But we still had a tough job ahead with the score level at 1–1. We needed another goal and it was proving extremely tough, with both sides lifting the intensity and hungry for a win.

'Come on Dunbar, keep up the pressure,' Coach James yelled.

Deep into the second half we were battle-weary, and a lapse in concentration nearly saw us concede another goal. Queens Park came close to wrapping up the game in the final five minutes. We looked on in horror as a looping ball floated in the air towards the upright corner of the net, beating our keeper, who was off his line. The ball hit the bar and then awkwardly dropped to the ground just a fraction off the goal line. Their substitute rushed in to finish it off, but Felix somehow managed to scoop the ball safely into his arms. How it didn't go in I'd never know. It was a gallant effort. I think we all had our hearts in our mouths.

With just a minute to go before the full-time whistle, Dylan made a break and off-loaded to Morgan, who danced his way past two defenders and into a gap. He raced towards the goal while I kept up with him.

'Go on, Morgan. Stay with him, Zeezou,' Coach James roared.

He made it to just metres outside the box as the defenders desperately snapped at his heels. I ran in behind him as he was about to shoot, ready to collect a possible rebound, while the keeper lunged forward in an attempt to stop Morgan's shot. But instead of shooting, Morgan sent me a clever back pass. With the keeper out of position, it seemed an easy task to send the ball past him. I struck the ball, watching it go in the right direction, but in the process a wayward last-minute sliding tackle caused me to lose my balance. I fell on my back.

I hadn't seen him coming . . . the defender's boots missed the ball and came crashing down on my head. All I could feel was heavy throbbing and then nothing. The next thing I knew, I was flying . . .

'Lucy, Zeezou, wake up, wake up.' 'Is she all right?'

'Oh no, the back of her head is covered in blood!'

I could hear lots of voices, shouting and yelling instructions. And then, suddenly, I heard Harry's voice.

'Lucy, you did it. You're one of us. You're a Lion, Zeezou!'

# Chapter 9

# Blackout

I was looking down a tunnel filled with an incredible light. I felt weightless and warm, drifting towards an enticing golden vision. Nothing else mattered and nothing else existed. I'd never seen or experienced anything like this before. I kept moving closer and closer to this inviting glow, until a soft voice roused my attention.

'Lucy, Lucy, wake up.'

It gave me a sudden jolt, inviting me back to reality, but the sensation of being cradled in an out-of-this-world experience kept tempting me. It's what I imagined floating and flying among the clouds would be like: weightless and free.

A quavering voice kept calling me. 'Lucy, please wake up. Come on. Wake up.'

Whatever was happening was incredible. No one would believe me if I told them. They'd think I was nuts. I slowly opened my eyes. Everything was blurry and my head was banging with pain. The throbbing subsided for a moment when I locked onto Harry . . . it was an awkward moment.

'Oh no, Harry, the game. What happened? Where am I?' I couldn't believe how weak my voice sounded.

Harry was relieved. 'Lucy, you're at your grandparents' flat. Thank heavens you're awake. I'm so sorry I was mean to you. I'm just not used to girls playing football. Your grandpa would have killed me if anything happened to you.'

'It's okay, Harry. Do my parents know what happened? They mustn't find out. Oh, my head is so sore. Did we win?'

Harry broke into a smile. 'Slow down! You took a hard knock from a nasty tackle. But we won, thanks to your last-minute goal.'

'The last thing I remember, we were on the football pitch and I was on the end of Morgan's back pass,' I muttered. I couldn't believe how badly my head was throbbing. I realised I was stretched out on the lounge in my grandparents' living room.

Grandpa came in from the kitchen, holding out a cup of tea. Harry stood up anxiously. 'Um, Mr Dib, I've got to head off. Take it easy, Zeezou. See ya!'

'Thanks Harry. See you at the Reg.'

'Grandpa, Mama doesn't know what happened, does she?' Tears sprang to my eyes at the thought. What if she found out – that would be the end of football. *Again.*

'I don't want you to worry about anything, Lucy,' Grandpa said. 'The main thing is that you're feeling better. It's nothing too serious. Luckily, Harry found me rather than Frida when he came with the news.'

'But are you sure she doesn't know? Mama will kill me if she finds out what happened on the pitch. If she knows I'm back playing football . . . my life is over.'

'Princess, I think you're being a little over-dramatic, calm down. She was visiting Nanna when Harry came. She's still there. You just need to rest and stop worrying!'

'Oh, thank you.' I was so relieved.

'You're welcome. The coach helped me bring you home and Morgan's mum is a doctor. She checked you and said it was a minor knock and nothing to worry about. She just instructed me to keep an eye on you. Rest is the remedy, so no football for a couple of days, and no dance classes.'

'But I feel much better already! I can't miss a session, I've only just made the team.'

'Lucy, you must rest. No football means no football. Don't get any ideas about sneaking to training, either, because I know everyone in the neighbourhood and they keep me posted on what's going on. I know you had a kick-around with young Max the other day – my spies are everywhere!' he joked.

'Max? You know Max? Why did he tell me his name was Roy?'

'Oh, Lucy, it's a long story. Max doesn't have a home. He lives in the back corner of the grandstand at the Reg. We all try to look out for him around here, but he won't accept much help.'

'Where are his parents?'

'They were killed about two years ago in a car accident.

Max is a ward of the state.'

'Oh my goodness. No parents . . . I can't imagine it. Poor Max. And he left our team because of me. I have to talk to him. I had no idea that he didn't have a home. That's awful, why didn't he tell me?'

'Max is a very proud boy. Roy's the name he uses to avoid being found out. He keeps running away from his foster homes and he refuses to stay in a refuge because he doesn't trust a soul. Now, that's enough about Max. You don't need to worry about him, or anyone else, right now. You need rest.'

I looked at him with concern. 'Grandpa, I don't know what to say. My problems don't seem that important any more. But what happens if Mama and Papa find out I'm playing again? That would be the end.'

'Princess, you are as dramatic as your mother and grandmother. I think it's great that you're chasing your dream. It's good to have a goal, but I don't really agree with keeping it a secret from your parents any longer.'

'I don't like it either, but I have no choice.'

'I can't see why Frida and Paolo don't want you to play football when it's their life and it's been a great part of your life too. Frida was encouraged to chase her dream across the globe. Surely she'd allow you to do the same, especially since you're so talented. Coach James thinks you have a very bright future in the game.'

'Oh, Grandpa, I needed to hear that. One day I'll be a great footballer – one of the best in the world,' I boasted. 'I'm sure you'll make it and I hope I'll be around to see you succeed. You know, I'd love nothing more than to watch my princess match it with the boys. Would you mind if I come along to your next game?' 'Sure, Grandpa, I'd love that.'

The pain in my head slowly subsided as my thoughts went back to Max. How did he sleep in a park all by himself? And like me . . . where did he fit in?

# Chapter 10

# School sux

Being the new girl on the block was never easy, and I knew that today, my first day at my new school, would be no different.

On arrival, Mama and I were greeted by the school captain and another student, who turned out to be Bella, the girl Mama told me about. On the way to the principal's office, Bella pulled me aside.

'Lucy, get ready to be humiliated on stage. The principal loves to show off her latest famous additions to the school … just grin and bear it.' We may have just met but we shared an instant connection.

'Thanks for the warning.'

After a brief meeting with the principal, Mrs Zambocelli, we were whisked off to the large assembly hall full of students, teachers and parents.

We were seated on the stage and then introduced gushily by Mrs Zambocelli. 'Girls, please welcome our new student, Lucia Zoffi. She's come all the way from Milan, Italy, and will be attending our fine school during her indefinite stay in Australia. Please do your best to make her feel welcome and a part of our wonderful school community.'

Mrs Zambocelli continued on her rant. 'This school prides itself on educating the girls from Australia's most respected and successful families. And it's today enriched by another distinguished family, revered in both the sporting and fashion worlds …'

Blah, blah, blah! How embarrassing. She knew all about my family's history and made a big deal out of it as she continued her introduction. I wondered if Mama had something to do with this show? This was right up her alley. We were just missing the string quartet to complete the occasion.

Would the principal also like to give them my shoe size? I was horrified by the disclosure of my personal details. I felt as if I was being paraded like a horse at the yearling sales. A crowd of unfamiliar faces stared and smirked at me, inspecting the new recruit.

Mama, however, was in her element, gleaming in the limelight, looking more like Posh Spice all dolled up for a photoshoot than a mother at a school assembly. I was missing Papa more than ever. I wished he was here. He would make light of this whole crazy scene. He knew how to make me laugh, and boy, did I need that right now.

And I knew that disaster lay ahead. The girls would either want to be my friend because of my parents' fame or hate me just because I'm a Zoffi. I could imagine what they were saying about me now:

'Who does she think she is?' 'Lucy or Lucia, who cares?'

'She's an amazon, but what's all the fuss about?' 'I love her mum's outfit, but too much make-up!'

I looked out for Bella, the only familiar face in a sea of strangers. I caught her signalling me at a side entrance. I couldn't wait to leave this nightmare and join her, but it wasn't over yet. Mama and I were special guests at the parents' morning tea. It was the first time I'd ever wished to be in class.

I thought things couldn't get any worse … but they did after morning tea. I'd completed a placement test last week and the results had secured me a spot in the class for gifted students, more commonly known as the nerd's class. Great, so now I was also a *nerd*.

The bell rang and Bella and I headed off to the nerds' class. Thank goodness I had Bella to explain the ins and outs of the school to me – what was cool, what wasn't. We'd make great team mates. I wondered if she played football. That would be perfect, but she didn't seem to be the sporty type. I still had a feeling we were going to become good friends. She'd already proved to be funny and easy to be around, just like Pino. Perhaps starting school here wasn't such a bad idea after all.

Looking around, I had to say that we were the coolest of the nerds, sitting at the back of the room and chatting away.

'I felt so sorry for you at the school assembly,' she said. 'I had the same humiliation in front of the school . . . it can make life here so hard.'

'It was a disaster. How could she do that to me?' I felt like pulling my hair out.

'Mrs Zambocelli thinks her introductions are in the best interest of the school and the students. She loves to brag about the number of influential families here, to make the school seem even more prestigious.'

'But doesn't she realise the trouble it causes? I like to keep a low profile, because in Italy we have no privacy. Does she do this to everyone? I can't –'

I was interrupted by a yell. 'Girls up the back . . . quiet! Pay attention. Bella Jones, you should know better. I will not tolerate any talking while I'm teaching my class and that also goes for our new student, Signorina Zoffi.' The teacher peered at me over her gold-rimmed glasses.

The rest of the class joined in with icy stares, and then the whispers and snide remarks erupted.

'Oooh, look who's made friends, mini-pollie and mummy's little model. What a pair of wannabes.'

'Jones and Zoffi, who would have thought they'd have anything in common?'

We scowled back and quietly continued our chat once they'd had enough and the teacher's attention was elsewhere.

'Yeah, all the high-profile families get the same treatment, although I think she gave you some extra gloss. My mum's the leader of a political party here, so I've also been embarrassed on that stage, but with less fanfare. Don't worry, I know what you're going through.' Now it made sense. 'That's why they called you mini-pollie?' Bella nodded.

'Wow, that's amazing. You must be so proud of her.'

'I am, but it's hard. I've had the hangers-on who want to know me just because she's a public figure, and others who just hate me because of their parents' politics. I get teased and left out sometimes. Mostly I keep to myself; I prefer it that way.'

'I know just how you feel . . . but don't most of these girls come from rich or famous families anyway?'

'Yes, but they're very competitive,' she explained. 'Everyone at this school wants to be the best. They're totally green with envy because you have a world-famous father. And being pretty doesn't help. And the fact that your mum was a model and still looks gorgeous just brings out the worst in them.'

'I wish my mama would dress down and not be so obsessed with fashion. If only they knew what my life is really like. My parents have these big plans for me that have nothing to do with what I want. Mama is pushing me to follow in her footsteps on the catwalk … boring!' 'Are you kidding? You're so lucky!' Bella looked at me, wide-eyed.

'No, you don't understand. I don't like it, strutting along the catwalk and posing for the cameras. I just wish I could be anonymous until I make my own mark, but with my family it's almost impossible. All I want to do is play football. That's my dream!'

'Football? Oh no, sport is boring, give me the catwalk any day … I love fashion.'

I hadn't expected that response.

Bella continued, 'Why on earth do you want to play football and get sweaty and dirty? My brother is a football fanatic but I'd never go to his games … now that would be boring! Lucy, you need to get your head read.'

'Thanks a lot! But seriously, you're the lucky one. I wish I had a brother who plays football. I'd train with him every day.'

Bella stared in disbelief. 'Really? You can have him. He's a pain in the butt. He's my twin but we don't have anything in common and thankfully we don't look alike. You'd probably like him – all he talks about is football.'

He sounded great to me.

'But a girl who loves football is a bit intriguing. How did you become obsessed with the silly game?' Bella laughed at my enthusiasm.

'Football's in my blood. I've been playing since I could walk. It's like a magical escape. There's nothing like running free and dancing with the ball until you reach the goal. Nothing else makes me feel that way. And I owe it to my Nonno Dino, who taught me to play. He used to say that one day I'd carry the Zoffi name into the next generation of football greats. And one day I will.'

Bella shook her head. 'I would never have thought that someone like you would be into chasing a ball with a bunch of jocks. You don't look like a football player, you're far too glamorous. Your mum's right, you should be a model.'

I shrugged, but Bella was on a rant. If only she knew there was a lump on the back of my head the size of an egg from the game the other day. My hair covered it, but it was still painful when I touched it. Glamorous – hardly!

'Modelling would be a great career. You can make loads of money, travel the world and hang out with movie stars, always looking fabulous.' She fluttered her eyelashes and blew a kiss to an imaginary camera. 'And then there's the beautiful designer clothes you get to wear.'

'Believe me, it's not as glam as it looks. It can be very bitchy and competitive . . . some girls snatch outfits from another girl's rack and a cat fight starts. Sometimes at the last minute a big-name celebrity decides they want to be in the show and all hell breaks loose. Okay, so maybe the catwalk can be fun, but it's still not my thing,' I conceded.

Bella pouted. 'I'd love to strut along a catwalk in designer clothes, but a curvy girl like me with glasses and braces wouldn't even get a look-in.'

'Oh, yes you would, Bella. You're beautiful, you live up to your Italian name,' I said.

'Oh, thanks,' Bella blushed. 'But you're the gorgeous one. I suppose you have to follow your own dream, though, and that takes guts.'

'How about you, what's your dream?' I asked.

'I'd love to model but there's no way my mum would support me. She wants me to go to uni because she thinks I'd be a good lawyer. Not interested! I know one thing for sure: there's no way I'd follow in her footsteps. I've seen what's expected in the world of politics and it consumes her whole life.' Bella finished quietly, 'She lives and breathes it and there's no room for much else.'

'I know what you mean. The only times I see my papa are when I go to his games, or sometimes when he's home for dinner, which isn't often. This isn't going to sound nice, but I love it when he's injured, because he has more time to spend with me.'

Bella laughed. 'Oh, wow, that's desperate!'

'While he's recovering, sometimes he'll take me to the football club to catch up with his team mates and manager. I love it because all they talk about is football, and there's no Mama.'

'No Mama? What's that supposed to mean?'

'Well, she's the one pushing me to model. And I have to compete for time with Papa because she dotes on him whenever the three of us are together … I'm lucky to get a word in. He's just always so busy with his football and their business. When family time comes along, it's always so rushed.'

'I know what it's like. My mum's always busy, and when she does get time with us it always seems to be interrupted by a crisis or media requests, even on the weekends. And as for my dad, well, he left a few years ago, but let's not go there. I totally understand how you feel, but Lucy, you're living every girl's dream. You've got it all!'

'I know I'm lucky, but it doesn't mean anything unless you can be who you want to be. I'm screaming to be me.' I waved my arms around like a true Italian. 'Luck doesn't mean anything unless you can do what you love. Football is the one thing I want to do more than anything, but I've been denied it. My parents banned me from playing about a year ago, but that hasn't stopped me playing with a team here – I just have to keep it secret. Please don't tell!'

Bella reassured me. 'Don't worry, Lucy, I won't tell a soul. Promise.'

We smiled and interlocked our little fingers.

'Girls! Bella and Lucy, that's enough! I told you no more talking. Detention for both of you,' yelled the teacher.

'But Miss …'

'No buts. I don't want to hear it. You'll both stay back after school. Now, not another word.'

# Chapter 11

# Love Lucy

Bella and I were lucky that time. Mrs Zambocelli was in the room when we showed up for our punishment. She didn't want her new celebrity pupil finishing her first day at the school with a detention, so after a quick telling-off, both of us were allowed to escape. We managed to be more discreet in class after that – it turned out Bella had a talent for passing notes undetected.

Things were going well with the Lions, too. We'd been training extremely hard and had won the last couple of games, bringing us even closer to holding up the revered trophy at the end of the season. If we won our next fixture we'd be the league's title holders and earn a spot in the Champion of Champions, a competition against the winners of all the leagues in the state.

Thankfully I made a full recovery from my knock to the head. I had to miss a couple of matches, which nearly drove me crazy. I felt fine, but Grandpa and Coach James were pretty stern about it – so I had to be content watching from the sidelines.

Now I was itching to play the vital next game against the Dolphins – it couldn't come soon enough. I could see it . . . tomorrow we'd be crowned Minor Premiers, the champions. I was imagining stepping up, holding the trophy, when Mama burst into the living room.

'Lucia, Lucia, I have some exciting news.'

'Mama, it's Lucy, remember? What's the news?' I was curious to find out what she was up to now.

'It will be Lucia again soon, my darling – we're going home for a few weeks!' she announced with great delight.

'That's wonderful, Mama, but when?' I was a little excited, but really, all

I could think about was the game.

'We leave tomorrow at eleven o'clock. I thought that since you have school holidays, we should make the most of them. I know it's short notice, but I've only just found out that our plane is here and available.'

I was horrified. 'But I have a game, I mean dance class, and I can't miss it. Why didn't you tell me sooner? How can we just get up and leave? What about Nanna and Grandpa?' I panicked, trying to weave my way out of this sudden dilemma.

'Calm down, Lucia. I thought you'd be excited! I've spoken to Grandpa and he understands. The best news of all is that Nanna is coming home today. I've organised a nurse to visit daily to check on her and a live-in housekeeper too, so they'll be well taken care of while we're away. And, darling, it's good to hear that you're so committed to your dancing,' she said gently, 'but missing a couple of classes isn't going to hurt.'

Oh, no, I couldn't believe it. I was thrilled that Nanna was coming home and I wanted to see Papa, but I couldn't miss the game. It was the most important game of my life so far. I didn't want to let my team down, especially since this would be my first game back after my injury. Since I'd been hanging out watching them train and going to their games, I was feeling like I was really one of them. This game was the team's most important fixture. How could Mama expect me to drop everything and go? I had to persuade her to delay the trip, at least by a day or so.

'But Mama, we have a concert coming up. It was supposed to be a surprise and it means so much to me to perform well,' I countered, hoping this might be enough to put off our departure.

'I'm glad you're so dedicated to dance, but you can catch up when we return. Besides, Papa is desperate to see you, and little Gigi misses you too. There's another surprise, which I wasn't supposed to tell you about just yet, but I can't wait any longer. I know that this will change your mind. We're launching our teen range and Papa's named it after you – it's called Love Lucy. You're the face of our new label!'

I looked at Mama. This was the kind of thing she lived for. She was practically glowing with enthusiasm. But I couldn't match her excitement. 'What? It would have been nice if you asked me first. I don't want to be the face of a fashion label and I don't want to go home tomorrow.'

Her face dropped. 'Don't be so ungrateful. It's an honour to have a fashion line named after you. It was going to be called "Love Lucia" but I told Paolo that you prefer to be called Lucy and he reluctantly agreed, just to keep you happy. And this is how you respond?'

I stood with my arms folded, trying to hold back my fury. 'But Mama, you don't understand –'

She snapped, 'No, you don't understand. You should think yourself lucky, young lady, as very few people are given an opportunity like this. It's your very own range, we did this for you, so start appreciating what you've got and stop whingeing.'

'It's your dream, not mine, Mama! Have you ever thought about asking me about what I want? No, you're so caught up in what you want for me. My life is ruined and it's all your fault.' I stormed off to the bedroom in hysterics.

I was lying on the bed covered in tears and crumpled tissues when I heard Grandpa come into the next room and say something in low tones to my mother. My ears pricked up and I crept over to the door, intent on listening to the unfolding conversation.

'Frida, I overheard your argument with Lucy. You could have delivered the news a little more gently,' Grandpa suggested.

'Dad, are you serious?' I could imagine Mama giving Grandpa her best glare. 'This is exciting news. She doesn't realise how lucky she is. A trip back home for a few weeks and the opportunity to be the face of our teen label – anyone else would be thrilled! But not my daughter, she goes nuts instead. She's too spoilt. I could only dream of a chance like this at her age and she just throws it back in my face. She's so ungrateful!'

'That was your dream, but maybe it's not hers. Why don't you sit down with her and explain what you're doing? She's fourteen years of age and fighting for her independence. You were pretty much the same at her age, you have to admit. Think about it from her point of view,' Grandpa explained gently. 'She's made some new friends and she's starting to settle in and suddenly she's being whisked away at a moments' notice.'

'I thought she'd be excited. Who wouldn't be?' Mama still sounded astonished. Why couldn't she listen to Grandpa?

'Lucy has her own mind and her own dreams just like you. Why don't you compromise and leave later tomorrow or the following day? It'll give her more time to sort out a few things. Remember, Frida, we all want different things in life. We always encouraged you in your endeavours and look at what you've achieved. I'm so proud of you. Personally, I think you need to give Lucy some space to be her own person.'

'Well, we have to leave tomorrow. We have a very tight schedule to work with and Paolo needs the plane back as soon as possible. I suppose we could leave a little later. But Dad, I know that she'll be grateful later. She just doesn't get it right now. I still want her to realise that she has to make the most of the opportunities at her fingertips.'

'My advice is to find out what she wants in life instead of forcing her to adhere to your expectations.'

That was it, Grandpa. He was getting through.

'I only want the best for her . . . but don't worry, I'll sort her out. Anyway, I'm just so glad Mum's coming home today. I'm only sorry that we have to leave so quickly. I'm worried that she might struggle with her mobility – we'll have to look into buying a ground level home so she doesn't have to climb those stairs. You'd be more comfortable, too. Maybe it's time to retire? We'll talk about that more when we're back,' said Mama.

'Frida, I appreciate everything you're doing for us but I love this business and this place. I don't know what I'd do without it. We're not moving. You're a good daughter. I don't know what we'd do without you . . . but please just take it easy on my princess,' Grandpa appealed.

'It's okay, Dad, she'll come around. The other thing I wanted to tell you is that Paolo and I have been talking, and we're thinking about trying to make the move here more permanent, at least for a while. It relies heavily on what's happening with his football, but we're hoping that maybe we can spend half our time here and the rest in Italy,' said Mama.

Wow! That would be so cool. I'd have the best of both worlds, more time with my grandparents and new friends here, and still have my home in Milan. The best news was that Papa seemed close to retiring, which meant he'd have much more time for me.

'That sounds wonderful!' said Grandpa. 'Let's face it, your mother and I aren't getting any younger and we want to spend as much time as possible with you and our precious Lucy.'

I stepped out of the bedroom to face them.

'Lucy, come and sit down. I've decided that we can leave a few hours later so that you can spend some time with your friends and fit in your class before we fly out. What time will you be finished?' Mama said in a soft tone, putting her arm around me.

Now, this was awkward . . . another white lie. The final would kick off at 11.30 am and should finish by about 1.30 pm, which would also allow time for the trophy presentation.

Let's see if she really wanted to make amends, I thought to myself. I glanced over at Grandpa with a guilty look. He gave me a wink of reassurance.

'Can we leave around 3.30?' I pleaded with my fingers crossed.

'Gosh, Lucia, how long is your class? Surely it shouldn't take that long. It costs money to keep the jet on standby. How about 3.00?' asked Mama.

Grandpa interrupted. 'Lucy, that sounds like a good deal. Why don't you start packing so you're ready to go straight after the game – I mean class?' He threw me a cheeky look.

'Hold on you two. Game? What game are you talking about?' Mama looked at us suspiciously.

'I think Grandpa was just getting mixed up with the big international game he wants to watch on TV tomorrow. Come on, Grandpa, don't we have some shelves to stack? I can start packing my bags later on.'

'Oh yes, princess . . . thanks for reminding me. I'm getting a little absent-minded these days,' Grandpa replied. I think he was enjoying the game we were playing.

But Mama was still suspicious. 'What's going on here?'

I jumped in, 'Nothing, we just want to make sure everything looks good before Nanna comes home.'

She was finally satisfied. 'Okay, it's settled then . . . we'll leave for the airport at three on the dot.'

'And Mama, I'm honoured to be the face of the Love Lucy label,' I said, to keep her happy.

She nodded, delighted. Grandpa and I ran downstairs to the shop armed with big smiles . . . mission accomplished.

Hi, Bella. Crazy news. Have to leave 4 Italy 2morrow. Wld u like 2 watch my ftball game b4 I fly out? Only time 2 catch up. Luv Lucy xxx

What? Why u going so soon?

Long story.

How long r u away 4?

All school hols.

U kno I don't like ftball but will come. Time?

Kick-off 11.30 @ the Reg.

Odd? My bro's playing @ same time @ Reg.

Maybe he's in the other team. Weird.

Yeah, c u then, B xxx Great! Ciao xxx

I was thrilled that Bella was coming to watch the game – I really wanted to see her before I left. Besides, hopefully it would get her interested in the sport. We'd been hanging out a lot at school. I tried not to talk too much football and she tried not to talk fashion – we had a lot in common, otherwise. I think it was because we were in a similar predicament with our families. After all, politics and sport weren't that different.

Bella knew what it was like to be isolated. She endured a hard time at school because she was the daughter of a public figure and very smart, verging on genius. She was self-conscious about her glasses and her body, but for no reason. I suspected the girls were just jealous that she was gorgeous *and* smart. We both put up with mocking at school, but at least we had each other.

I was sure Grandpa would love her, too – I couldn't wait for her to meet him, and all the guys at the Reg.

'Look who's here,' Grandpa yelled, opening the door and pushing Nanna along in a wheelchair.

'Nanna, welcome home!' I gave her a careful hug and lots of kisses. It was so wonderful to see her home again.

'Mum, welcome home!' Mama cried.

'Thank you, my gorgeous girl. I've missed you. I missed all of you. I'm so happy to be home and even happier to have you and my Lucy here.' Nanna grinned, but had tears in her eyes.

She still looked fragile but at least she was on the road to recovery. We gently wheeled her inside and helped her out of the wheelchair, up the stairs and into her favourite armchair.

That night we spoiled her with a home-cooked meal, prepared by Mama and me. It was the first time we'd ever cooked together. I didn't even know Mama *could* cook, but she seemed to enjoy it and so did I. It was a rare moment for us, and I was surprised to find that we made a good team. Mama was even singing while stirring the pot, and performing funny dance steps. I hadn't seen that in a very long time.

When Mama finally went to bed, I stayed up and shared my secrets with Nanna. What she said gave me hope. 'One day your parents will come around. But most importantly, believe in yourself and stay focused. I know you can do it. Promise me that you'll never give up.'

# Chapter 12

# The matador and the bull

'Today, we're playing for the right to be crowned league champions. Let's get stuck in from the kick-off and force them onto the back foot. First to the ball from the whistle,' Coach James lectured us in the change room. We were all fidgety, with nerves setting in as game-time drew near, but Coach James knew how to settle his team. 'Let's forget about last night's hot dates and your fancy moves on the disco floor.'

There was an explosion of laughter. Disco?

'I want to see fancy footwork on the pitch! Dylan and Morgan, it's important that we support our strikers: you need to control the midfield to make sure Lucy and Harry see a lot of the ball. Then we'll have plenty of movement up front. Utilise Morgan's speed and look for each other. Dugald, Jasper, Taj and Jonathon, I want you to guard the back line with your life. Don't forget to get the ball out wide to Brandan and Jared. Most importantly, support each other. Communication is the key. I want to see a clean sheet today. Now, you all know what's at stake.' 'Yes, Coach, we're ready to take them on,' Brandan said, and we all nodded.

'Good, that's what I want to hear. So let's get out there and show them a united team that knows how to win. Most importantly, get out there and have some fun … but not too much.' Coach James gave us a big smile and wished us luck. We ran onto the pitch to the sounds of encouragement from the sidelines.

Suddenly a familiar voice stood out from the rest. 'Princess, good luck!'

I looked over and saw Grandpa watching proudly from the sidelines, wearing a huge smile.

'Oh, my little princess, don't dirty your pretty pale pink outfit. Come on, my princess, you can get past those bad, bad boys. Just don't mess up your hair,' a voice mocked from the other side of the pitch.

'Ha ha. Who's that scaredy-cat trying to make fun of me?' I demanded, trying to get a better look at him.

'Who else would it be, Zeezou? It's me . . . the best player on this pitch,' he boasted.

'I should have known it was you, Max . . . carrying on in such a childish manner. Look out, you'll be watching me zigzag straight past you in just a moment. Then we'll see who ought to wear the tiara.'

'Oooh, it's Lucy Zeezou the comedian. You really have me worried. Let's catch up when I'm holding the trophy with my new team mates.' He stretched his arms out to mimic celebration.

'You can't stop us and you know it. Game on!' I trumpeted.

Just before the whistle blew, Bella's voice interrupted the stand-off. 'Lucy, I need to talk to you.'

But the game was about to start, so whatever she had to tell me would have to wait. She really didn't seem to understand sport.

Even so, I was excited that she was here, and because this was the first time Grandpa had come to watch me. Nanna would have loved to come too, but she still needed plenty of rest. And anyway, she was helping by keeping Mama busy. I wished I didn't have to fly out today. I'd have loved to stay and hang out with the team after the game.

The whistle blew and we attacked from the outset. We started working our way down the pitch but we were all a little nervous, and I was finding it hard to focus.

'Lucy, what are you doing?' yelled Harry. 'Oh, sorry.'

'It's not like you to mistime a pass. Your head's in the clouds. Focus!'

'All right. No need to get shirty,' I bit back.

'Come on, let's lift our game,' Brandan demanded. 'Stop bickering and get on with it.'

'Lucy, play your way into the game,' Coach James instructed from the sidelines.

I was having a very ordinary first half so far. I was struggling to stay focused . . . there was too much going on. I had to regain my composure.

'Mark up,' Coach James yelled.

Oh no, too late! Our opponents had just sunk one into the back of the net, thanks to a superb strike from outside the box by their talented forward. The score was 1–0 to the Dolphins . . . Harry threw me a filthy look, and I returned a tough gaze, standing my ground.

'Come on, team. We can come back . . . we've just got to focus. Heads up,' urged Brandan.

'You can do it, princess. Come on, Dunbar!' Grandpa encouraged from among the crowd.

I could also hear Bella yelling at the top of her voice, 'Go Dylan, come on Lucy.'

Bella was yelling out support for Dylan. What was that about?

I miskicked yet another pass and sent it flying out of Jared's reach.

'Dunbar, we must keep possession,' bellowed Coach James. 'Lucy, come on, get onto the ball and let's see those goal-scoring boots.'

I had to pull myself together. It had been a long time since I had a family member barracking for me on the sidelines. Nonno Dino was always at my games when I was little, and it felt good to have Grandpa here today.

The ball came my way, thanks to good service from the midfield. I made a run and looped the ball back inside to Dylan. He delivered a beautiful pass back and then I put in a cross to Harry, who was free on the left. He volleyed the ball, connecting perfectly with his right foot and sending the ball into the top right-hand corner for the equaliser.

1–1. The Lions were back in business as the half-time whistle blew.

We walked off with a sense of satisfaction. It was a relief that we'd pulled one back, but we still had a lot of work to do if we were to win this game and the league. And I needed to pull my socks up or I'd be keeping the bench warm.

Coach James delivered the half-time talk. My head was down, as I was disappointed with my wayward performance. But Coach James remained positive as usual.

'Heads up, Zeezou, lads. Despite a slow start we're back in the game, but we need to keep more possession. Brandan, I like the way you're leading the players. Keep up the encouraging words. Defenders, let's get tighter at the back and talk to each other.'

Dugald interrupted, 'We need to get stuck in and stop the fancy stuff, just pass the ball.'

'You're right. Zeezou, Harry, good work in the last five minutes but I want to see that throughout the rest of the next half. No more chatter and more focus on your roles. I know some of you are distracted by Max playing for the other team, but let's just get on with it. We're not far away from a good result, as long as we keep our minds on the job.'

Harry interrupted. 'I can't wait to beat that traitor.' 'Hey, now.' Coach James frowned. 'That's an attitude

I don't want. We're playing against a team and Max is just another player. Now, I'm going to make a few changes in the second half. Anyone tired?'

'NO!' we chorused, all determined to stay on and finish the job.

'Remember, one step at a time. Another goal and we're on our way to the Champion of Champions. I believe in you. So let's go, Dunbar Lions, let's go!'

Coach James pulled me aside. 'Zeezou, is everything okay? You seem a little distracted out there.'

'Sorry, Coach. It's the first time Grandpa and my friend Bella have come to watch. I'm not used to having my own support on the sidelines and hearing my name called out. But don't worry. I know what to do. Zeezou's back.'

'I have confidence in you. Now get out there and show me your best so that we have something to celebrate. Either way, I'm going to take the team out for pizza afterwards.'

'Oh no, I can't come! We're flying back to Italy straight after the game. I'm sorry I haven't told you earlier but I only found out yesterday,' I replied, disappointed.

'That's one way to get out of training next week! Lucky you, off to Europe. We can celebrate when you return. How long are you going for?'

'We're away all of the school holidays, maybe a bit longer. I'm really upset about missing games in the tournament, but I have no choice.'

'We're going to miss your skills, but hopefully you can make it back in time for the final. I'm being very confident, of course, about our pending win today. Now, the whistle's about to blow and right now I want you switched on.'

We ran back on for the second half. This time, I could hear Grandpa and Bella expressing their support but I didn't acknowledge them. I just looked straight ahead and kept my eyes on the ball. I knew that Grandpa would understand, but Bella probably wouldn't. I could imagine the conversation, with Bella hurt and confused that I wasn't waving back:

'What's wrong with Lucy, Mr Dib?'

'Well Bella, she's just putting her head down and bum up. She means business . . .'

Harry stood unusually close and whispered, 'Lucy, we can get another one. Look out for me, I'm going to surprise them. Max will regret ever leaving us.'

'Okay, but please forget about Max. Just give me the signal and I'll be there to back you up,' I said.

We kicked off and found ourselves on the back foot right from the start. The Dolphins had come out determined, attacking early and pushing their way up the pitch.

Even so, Dugald had the back line under control until one of their strikers surprised him with a shimmy to find space. He came close to giving the Dolphins an early lead in the second half, with a shot on target.

Thankfully, Felix was having a good game. He leapt to the ball to make a great save. He cradled the prize in his arms, to our relief.

We traded chances for the next twenty minutes, neither team relenting until Harry finally found a way through. Jared spotted his run and unleashed a long ball which headed to Harry's feet with pinpoint accuracy. He outmanoeuvred the defenders in his path and set himself up to take a shot on goal. But he hadn't seen what was heading his way.

'Man on, Harry!' I yelled at the top of my lungs.

We looked on in horror: we could see what was about to happen. Max was charging towards him like an unstoppable steam train. He caught Harry off guard and collected him like a vulture honing in on its helpless prey. Harry was taken out by the full force of Max's tackle and fell heavily on his back while Max cleaned up the ball and sent it back to his midfielders. I was so furious – surely it was a foul? Max had struck Harry from behind with his studs showing, but to my astonishment the referee played on.

There were shouts of dissent from the sidelines. 'That was a dangerous tackle.'

'Ref, he could have broken his legs.' 'Penalty!'

But they fell on deaf ears as play continued up the pitch. I ran out of my position and chased after Max, but luckily for him I was instructed to return up front. 'Lucy, don't retaliate. We fight for the ball not the player!' yelled Coach James.

With just five minutes remaining and the score locked at 1–1, we quickly worked the ball back up to our end of the pitch again. I looked out for Harry and spotted him still lying on the ground.

I screamed, 'Kick the ball out. Harry's still on the ground.'

Jasper was running with the ball. He kicked it out and the referee blew his whistle. We ran over to check on Harry, including Coach James. His left boot was delicately taken off to reveal a swollen ankle and grazes seeping blood along his legs.

'That scumbucket. Look at what he did. I'm going to sort him out,' he grimaced.

'Harry, calm down. It was a very heavy tackle but I don't think Max meant to hurt you. Unfortunately I'm going to have to take you off. It looks as though you may have twisted that ankle, and it needs some ice. Look on the bright side – you didn't lose a foot, just a boot,' Coach James joshed.

'Very funny, Coach, but I think I can still play,' Harry insisted. He attempted to stand but quickly crumbled back to the ground. He had no choice but to leave the pitch.

I tapped him on the shoulder and whispered, 'Don't worry, Harry. We'll sort it out on the pitch.'

Now we were even more determined to take the game to them and perform like champions. Kurtis came on for Harry, eager to make his mark. 'We have to take them by surprise. Coach James wants the defenders to push up, use our set piece and storm the box with all bodies. Whoever has a chance must seize the opportunity and strike. Jonathon, he wants you to stay back in case they break through. The rest of us need to go for it. Time's running out.'

'Lions, we can do it,' Brandan yelled.

We managed to fight our way up the pitch as Kurtis negotiated his route towards the opposition's goal. He beat three players and off-loaded to me. I zigzagged my way through and passed to Dugald, who surprised our confused rivals as he pushed forward. He spotted Jasper on the run and sent the ball just ahead of him. Jasper gained possession and let all his tricks out of the bag, leaving the defenders in his wake. Unmarked, he cracked the ball from outside the box straight past the keeper, but it hit the crossbar. The box was full of bodies but I managed to time my run perfectly. I collected the rebound with a scissor kick that sailed past the disoriented keeper for the winner, right on the full-time whistle. The Dunbar Lions had secured a spectacular 2–1 victory. I exploded into a series of dance moves and finished with a pirouette and a bow to our ecstatic supporters.

I think my celebrations may have caused more of a stir than the winning goal. It didn't matter, I was one of the boys and they let me know it by lifting me onto their shoulders and chanting, 'Zeezou, Zeezou, Zeezou!'

Coach James burst onto the pitch with a satisfied smile, cheering and congratulating us. 'I'm so proud of my lions and lioness. It was a joy to watch you play such good attacking football. I knew you could do it. Brilliant!' Then he led the cheers for our bitterly disappointed opponents. 'Three cheers for the Dolphins . . . hip, hip, hooray, hip, hip hooray, hip, hip hooray.'

They reciprocated and we all shook hands.

To my great surprise, Max came over and congratulated me. He looked deep into my eyes. 'A cracker of a goal, Zeezou,' he said.

'Um, thanks Max,' I mumbled, feeling a little uncomfortable.

'I didn't mean any harm earlier, I was just having a bit of fun. Hope to see you down at the Reg one day.'

'Sure, Max. Unlucky today. See you soon,' I said, melting into his big brown eyes.

That was strange – he wanted to see me again and I kind of thought I'd like that. I didn't know what was going on, but I felt a little weird. We were very much alike in some ways, but in others very different. I thought again about Max being homeless and wondered if I could help him somehow, but then I was distracted by the celebrations around me.

The team was still jumping, singing and dancing, but it came to an abrupt end. Harry caught everyone by surprise when he limped over to Max, who was still standing on the pitch. Without hesitation or warning, Harry gave him a right hook, knocking him to the ground. Max curled up on the ground holding the side of his face while Harry towered over him yelling, 'You idiot! You took me out on purpose. Now, let's see how you like being chopped down and humiliated, you little coward.'

'Oooh, we'll see about that,' said Max, rising to his feet with fists poised for action.

The other boys looked on in surprise. Dylan yelled, 'That's enough, just shake hands and get over it.' But his call for a truce was ignored.

This was definitely one time I was glad to be a girl. I didn't mind getting physical on the pitch but fighting is uncivilised, especially in sport. 'Guys, stop it. You've got to stop it!' I screamed in desperation.

But it fell on deaf ears. Max was stamping like a bull in a ring, nostrils flaring, sizing up his opponent, ready to strike. Harry didn't even need to tease him with the red matador's bolero, although he would have been better off waving the white flag.

It all happened so quickly. Max leapt at Harry, expelling a thunderous roar and headbutting his old friend, who crashed to the ground.

Coach James came sprinting out from the change room but he was too late; the damage was done. He attended to the injured matador moaning in pain, while the victorious bull made his escape.

I don't know what came over me but I suddenly found myself chasing Max.

'Max, wait! Please Max, wait!' I yelled urgently.

'Wait for what? No one understands me. I had to defend myself! I'm out of here,' he screamed, as he kept running.

I desperately tried to reach him, but he was too fast. I stopped at the top of the street, hoping to get a glimpse of him and wondering if I'd ever see him again. I felt sick in the stomach.

Dylan called after me, 'Lucy, wait . . .' When he caught up with me, we sat on the fence. 'What are you doing? Why are you chasing Max? He's a talented footballer but he's a psycho.'

'I thought I could try to talk to him. I'm the reason he left our team, so I feel responsible for this mess,' I explained, still looking up the street for any sign of him.

'You know, we've played football with him for years now, but we still don't know much about him. He's just very private. And I don't want to be around the next time he and Harry see each other,' said Dylan.

'How is Harry?' I asked.

'He'll be fine. It's more pride than pain. He wants to see you. He's worried you've already left for Italy without saying goodbye. C'mon, let's go back.'

'Oh no! The plane! I can't be late. I've got to go or I'll be in big trouble!' I started to panic.

'Why can't you stay and celebrate? Why do you have to leave so soon?' Dylan sounded a little upset. I looked up in surprise and saw that his cheeks had turned rosy.

'The plane has to leave in a few hours, so I don't have long to get organised,' I said, standing up. 'I can't wait to see my papa and my dog, Gigi, but I'm devastated that I'm going to miss most of the Champion of Champions tournament. Hopefully I'll be back for the final. Please make sure that we make it!'

We started to walk back towards the others.

'Don't worry, Lucy, we'll get to the final. We're good enough to win it. Are you planning to catch up with your friends in Italy?' he asked, catching me by surprise.

'Oh, um, I'm not sure. I haven't had time to think about it. I have a few football friends that I'll probably hang out with, but I want to spend as much time as I can with my papa and Gigi. Why?'

'No reason, just wondering,' Dylan replied coyly. 'Lucy, hey Lucy!' Bella came running towards us. 'I'm so sorry, Bella! I've got to go. I'm running late for my flight,' I said.

'But we haven't had a chance to catch up! I still don't know what all the fuss is about, but congratulations.' Bella looked at Dylan. 'Hey, good game.'

'How do you two know each other?' I asked, remembering that she had supported him on the pitch.

'Oh, sorry Lucy, that's what I wanted to tell you earlier.

This is my brother.'

'You're kidding! That's so crazy! I wish I could stay and hang out, but I've got to leave right now. Sorry, but Mama's already put the flight back a few hours.' I hoped they'd understand.

Bella stepped in. 'Okay, but quickly tell me, what on earth happened out there? This is why I don't like sport. It's full of thugs and crazy people, present company excluded of course. Although . . . that guy you were chasing was cute. Who's he?'

Dylan rolled his eyes. 'Don't you remember Max Spitzer?'

'Max? Was that really Max? Wow. He used to have long dirty hair. That new haircut's made all the difference.' Bella looked at me and smirked.

Thankfully we were interrupted by Grandpa shouting. 'Come on Lucy, we must leave immediately. Your mum is waiting.'

'I'm coming, Grandpa.' I turned to Dylan and Bella. 'Sorry I have to race off, but I'll text you as soon as we land. I'm not going to have time to say goodbye to Harry. Please tell him I'm so sorry but if I don't leave now my mama will go psycho!' We hugged quickly and then I raced off with Grandpa.

We made it back to the shop without a minute to spare. Mama was enjoying a final chat with Nanna as I ran in and gave them both a kiss.

We grabbed our suitcases and were ready to go, but then Mama's phone rang.

'Lucy, can you get that, please? I left it upstairs on the coffee table.'

I ran up and grabbed it. 'Hello, Lucy speaking.'

'It's great to hear your voice, my beautiful girl. I called to say I can't wait to see you and I have a few surprises waiting for you. Gigi also misses you.'

I could hear her barking in the background. I couldn't wait to hold my little Gigi.

'Papa! I miss you, I can't wait to see you either. But I have to go, we're running late.' It was so good to hear his voice.

'Okay, Lucy. Lots of kisses. I love you. Can you please put Mama on?'

'Of course. See you soon! Love you, ciao.'

Mama pounced on the phone, sounding all giggly, like a schoolgirl talking to her first boyfriend. It was funny to watch her in action.

I gave her some privacy and joined Nanna and Grandpa.

'Nanna, I'm so glad you're out of hospital. I just wish we weren't leaving now, I want to spend more time with you. My team won the match today – I couldn't have done it without you and Grandpa supporting me. Thank you!' 'Congratulations, sweetheart. And don't you worry . . .

I plan to spend all my time with you when you return.' Nanna squeezed me tightly, then whispered, 'Don't worry, Lucy. We'll talk my stubborn Frida around somehow.'

'Thank you, princess,' Grandpa said. 'Now let's get your mother off the phone or your pilot may miss his clearance. Then there'll be trouble.'

Mama came down the stairs, still gasbagging to Papa.

'Frida, it's time to go. You'll be seeing your husband soon enough,' said Grandpa, as the driver came in to take our bags to the car. She blew kisses into the phone and finally hung up.

We all hugged as the tears started to roll. I couldn't believe it – I'd just started to settle here and I was off again. 'Don't worry, we'll be back before you know it,' said Mama, who looked as if she'd surprised herself with such an emotional departure.

Once we were in the car, I realised I didn't even know where we were heading first. 'Mama, where are we going, Milano or Lake Como?'

'First stop is Milano. Papa is at the Milanello training grounds preparing for a game, although he'll be able to join us at home for the first week. That's when we'll work on the Love Lucy photoshoot.'

'Great, it'll be so much fun.' I tried to inject some enthusiasm into my voice.

Mama, on the other hand, couldn't contain herself. 'It's so exciting, my daughter the face of our teen label. I can't wait to get to the studio and see you work your magic in front of the camera again. It's been a while.'

Yeah . . . I couldn't wait!

'And if you like, Papa said you can watch him in the local derby on the following Sunday. This time I'll come with you. I haven't seen him play for a while. I should show my face! And we'll make sure that we spend some time relaxing at Lake Como. And of course we must go shopping . . .' By this stage Mama was on a roll. 'I miss the Galleria Vittorio Emanuele and Via Della Spica, and I can't wait to dine at Cracco Peck again. We're also going to catch up with Giorgio. I need a new gown for a ball we're attending. I can't wait to get back home,' she announced with a huge smile.

Never mind the shoot, I was bubbling with excitement about the game. Watching the local derby between AC Milan and Inter was my favourite thing, besides actually playing.

We arrived at the waiting jet without a minute to spare. Our passports were checked while another officer combed over our things with a metal detector. The flight attendant greeted us warmly.

'Good afternoon, Signora and Signorina Zoffi, welcome aboard. Please take your seats for immediate take-off.'

# Chapter 13

# Papa's princess

I hadn't realised quite how much I'd missed Papa until he entered the room. His thick brown hair was swept back and his green eyes crinkled up with his huge smile. You couldn't help but love him.

I greeted him with a matching smile, knowing that I had him all to myself while Mama dolled herself up to make her grand entrance. I ran into his arms, hugging him tightly. I couldn't contain my excitement.

'Papa, I missed you so much. Did you beat Roma?

What was the score? I'm coming to your next game.'

'That's what I love about you, Lucia, your lust for life. Of course I missed you, my darling girl. And yes, we did win – but more importantly, look at you,' he said dotingly, caressing my cheek. 'I'm so proud that you're going to be the face of Love Lucy.'

'I love the sound of it, Papa. It's an honour', I said, trying to hide my disappointment that he wanted to talk about that straight away. Oh well, I wasn't into the fashion thing, but I was extremely touched that he and Mama had named the label after me.

'We've organised your favourite photographer, Enzo, for the shoot, so it will be lots of fun. And this time, since it's featuring you, I've asked him to mix fashion with sport. It's more suited to the youth market. I haven't told your mama about that yet . . . let's surprise her. We may even use a football in the shoot. What do you think, gorgeous?'

I was completely taken by surprise. Did Papa know that I'd been playing football again, or was this some lucky coincidence? Finally, I could really enjoy a photo-shoot.

'Yes, I think it's a great idea, Papa,' I responded carefully. 'I'm sure kids my age will love it. And I promise I'll do my best at the shoot and make you proud.'

'I'm already proud of you Lucia, I mean, Lucy. Mama told me you are doing very well at your new school and your dancing classes. She mentioned something about a dance concert in Sydney that you're performing in soon. You know I can't promise anything, but I'll try my best to be there. It's about time I took a trip to Australia.'

'Oh, Papa, really? That would be great.'

'And you've been doing a great job helping your grandpa. He tells me that you've made some good friends, although he did let it slip that they're mostly boys. You know you're too young to be interested in boys.' His eyebrows knitted together as he threw me a concerned look.

'Papa! I'm not interested in boys, I just like hanging out with them. Anyway, I've made a very good friend at school, called Bella.'

'Ah, that's good to hear.'

'She's a bit of a bookworm but we get on very well. And she's the daughter of a politician. Your club president knows her family.'

'Well, I like the sound of a friend who has her head in books . . . it's the best place for girls, especially mine. You should spend more time with her rather than the boys. They're trouble – believe me, I was young once and I know what they're like.' He gave me a cheeky grin.

'It's not like that, we're just friends. We have a lot in common,' I replied.

'But what can you have in common with a bunch of boys? You love fashion and modelling and girly things like your mama. That's what I love about you. You're wise beyond your years, and sometimes very stubborn, but every inch a young lady.' He announced this proudly, while I crumbled inside at his vision of me. Maybe it was his way of holding on, pretending that I was still just a little kid.

Couldn't he see that I was different, especially from Mama? How could he be so off the mark? Maybe he just didn't want to recognise that his little princess was a tomboy. I didn't really fit into his ideal world. I was always in jeans or my favourite trackpants, but I suppose he didn't see that very often, since he was always playing football or keeping up with sponsorship commitments.

I could hear Mama bolting down the corridor. Her heels banged purposefully towards us, then she arrived looking radiant and immaculate, dressed in a low-cut, perfectly fitted red Valentino dress. Papa was extremely pleased to see her – his eyes goggled out of his head as she threw herself into his welcoming arms. They embraced and started to get mushy . . . yuck, yuck, yuck, I was out of there. I went to make my exit, but Papa wrestled himself away from Mama.

'Lucia, er, Lucy, wait. I have something for you. I'll be back in a minute – stay right where you are,' he ordered. He soon returned carrying a big box covered with a blanket. I couldn't work out what it was until I heard a familiar noise.

'Gigi, my little Gigi. Oh, I've missed you,' I blurted, feeling tears come to my eyes. Papa opened the box and my chihuahua jumped into my arms, covering my face with welcoming licks. Gigi and I had a lot of catching up to do. Cuddling her now reminded me of Nonno Dino, because he'd bought her for me on my sixth birthday.

I started to relax as I headed to my room with Gigi. It was great to be home again – I was a lot more excited than I'd thought I'd be. Then I remembered: usually at this time of day the boys would be playing football at our local park. I decided it was time to put on the boots and unleash the real Lucy. Jet lag would have to wait.

I quickly packed my bag with my football gear and Gigi, and shouted, 'I'm just going up the road for a gelato with a few friends.'

'Okay, we'll go out for *aperitivi* then,' Mama said. 'Why don't you meet us at our usual place for dinner later? Call us when you're ready, but don't be too late. We'll leave the driver with you.'

'Oh no, that's okay, I'll be fine.'

Mama quickly bounced back, 'No, it's not up for discussion. We still have to be careful – we're not taking any risks, and that's final.'

Mama might have been glad to be back in Milano, but the freedom she'd given me in Sydney was starting to slip away.

'Come on, Pino, pass the ball . . . what are you doing?' I yelled out. I'd managed to shake off our driver. He was happy to have the night off.

Pino kicked the ball out and ran over with the rest of the boys. 'Ciao, Lucy! Good to see you back home. How long are you staying?'

'Just a few weeks, I think. I'm desperate for a game, can I play?'

He nodded.

We got stuck in and played for a couple of hours, as if I'd never left. That was the great thing about football: words weren't necessary. Even Gigi enjoyed it, barking like crazy. It felt so good being on my home turf, but deep down I knew that this could be the last time I got to kick around with the boys for a long time. I was in my element, loving every minute of the game.

'Zeezou, you're on fire. Sydney must agree with you!' Pino yelled after I scored my third goal.

I couldn't get enough. I passed the defenders with ease, stalking like a panther towards the goal. I was on a mission, thinking about how I could get my papa's approval. I wanted to show him the footballer within, I wanted him to see Lucy Zeezou.

After the game we went to our local hangout, a gelato bar across the road from the park. We talked about Sydney and its football scene as I ate my favourite chocolate gelato, and Gigi enjoyed her own version.

A sudden flash of light distracted me momentarily, but I was too involved in the football discussion to pay attention. Then one of the boys yelled, 'Hey you, get out of here.'

# Chapter 14

# Famous life

Now that we were back, Mama was caught up in her own world again, frantically organising her schedule to catch up on all the latest gossip with her friends over long lunches and dinners. There were a few society events to attend, and of course appointments for fittings with her favourite designers. She was practically frothing at the mouth knowing she was back in the limelight, living her dream life. Going back to Sydney would be a challenge for her.

The paparazzi had already snapped us walking along the Piazza del Duomo together. They were mainly after Papa the football legend. He just managed to put up with it, and I tried to ignore them, but Mama loved it, always armed with a pout for the camera. It was like being constantly followed by a pack of hungry sharks.

Today though, the photographers would be on our side. Papa and I were heading to the Love Lucy shoot. Thankfully, Mama was going to catch up with us later. This gave me some time to hang out with Papa . . . well, if you could call a photoshoot time together.

'Ciao, Lucia, it's been too long, the camera and I have missed you,' gushed Enzo. He put his hands on my shoulders and stood back. 'Let me have a good look at you. My, you've grown into an even more beautiful young lady. And what's in the water in Australia? You're suddenly taller than me!'

'That wouldn't be hard, Enzo', I said with a cheeky smile. 'But as usual, you're too charming. Papa says the shoot is going to be different, with more of a sporty theme?' I walked around the studio to get a feel for the shoot.

'I have a few fun ideas for this campaign but I want to surprise you. I know you love the girly thing, but this could be a new look. I think you'll make the Love Lucy label hugely successful, especially now that there's going to be a massive billboard campaign across Europe. You must be so excited! Now,' he continued his rant, 'let's get you into hair and make-up. Anastasia is waiting for you.' 'What billboards? Papa, you didn't tell me I'd be seen all over Europe!' I was shocked at the thought.

'Isn't it exciting? We've already sold the label to most of the European capitals and we're close to securing a deal in the US and possibly Australia too,' he announced proudly.

I almost couldn't bear to say anything. 'But Papa, my friends will give me such a hard time. I can't be splattered all over the place. They'll think I'm a show-off.'

'Lucia, you've grown up in front of the camera and in the public eye. And besides, I know you'll love it when you see the designs. Enzo is going to make the shoot a lot of fun for you.' Papa made himself comfortable on the lounge and picked up his macchiato.

Before I had a chance to say anything more, Anastasia came running into the room. 'Ciao, young lady. Let's go! While I'm putting your face on, the stylist can give you a peek at the new designs. The clothes are very groovy and beautifully made. I think you'll love them.'

I sat back while the stylist showed me the range. I was pleasantly surprised. The Love Lucy clothes were actually my style: sporty yet smart casual gear you could wear on all occasions. Some of the outfits were a bit too glittery for my taste, but I loved the design on the T-shirts and singlets – a love heart with my name scrawled alongside it in ruby red, or different colours to suit your taste.

I had to admit the label was brilliant, especially the jeans and cool T-shirts. I also liked the bomber jackets, which had the heart design scrawled across the back. There was even a range of reversible tracksuits. It didn't seem to be Mama's style, but I loved the range instantly. I was starting to feel like one of the fashion queens I detest. I needed to get back onto the pitch, and quick!

After close to an hour and a half of hair, make-up and the stylist fiddling with the clothes, I was deemed ready to play for the camera. I walked into the studio, dressed in a sparkly silver top with a big red love heart splattered on the front, black fitted straight-leg pants with a zipper theme and big pockets, and a pair of cool red sneakers covered with little black hearts and sprinkles of silver.

'Lucia, all I can say is stunning. Stupendo!' yelled Enzo. 'See Enzo, I told you my beautiful girl was perfect for this label,' Papa gloated.

Enzo agreed and then snapped to it, directing me from behind his camera. 'Now Lucia, please move to the centre of the backdrop and just have fun. I want you looking as though you're messing around with one of your friends.'

I put on my best playful mood in front of Papa, trying to impress him. I occasionally looked over and winked or blew him a kiss.

'That's it, Lucia. Perfect. I want more of that.' Enzo nodded as he clicked furiously.

I savoured this moment, as ones like it didn't come around very often. I had Papa's full attention, and we were both enjoying ourselves.

My treasured time was cut short by his mobile ringing. He answered it, signalled he'd only be a minute, and then promptly left the room.

'Lucia, keep smiling and play up to the camera.'

Click, click, click. After a few minutes I was ushered away to change into a new outfit, and then began posing all over again. This time I wore the black T-shirt with the Love Lucy print and denim jeans. This was more like it. But I wished Papa was back.

'Nice outfit Lucy. I'd like to try something different. Your papa is a genius with the ball … now let's see what his daughter can do.' To my surprise, Enzo threw me a football while still snapping.

My two lives suddenly came together. I forgot where I was and totally immersed myself in my football world, juggling the ball and performing fancy tricks.

'*Mama mia*, Lucia, you are a vision to behold, poetry in motion. Never have I seen anyone so beautiful control a football with such ease and grace.'

I could hear Enzo but I wasn't listening. I was in the zone, acting on instinct. Just me and the ball, that's what made me happy.

The camera continued to click as I played to my heart's content, balancing the ball on the back of my head...rolling it down my spine and kicking it into the air with the back of my heel. I juggled the ball with my feet for a while and then sent it hurtling past the camera.

'Brilliant, Lucia! Now, dribble towards me and as you're about to reach me, go straight past, first left and then right,' Enzo yelled excitedly, trying to maintain the energetic mood and capture something special.

Click, click, click.

Enzo paused for a moment while his assistant handed me some netting and adjusted a few lights. 'Now, just hold the net in front of you and peer through it, as if you're about to attack your opponent.'

Snap, snap, snap.

'Fantastic! Now celebrate as though you've just scored a goal.'

That wasn't hard. It's what I did best. I was getting carried away but I couldn't help myself. I was obsessed ... or possessed – I wasn't sure which, but it was so much fun.

'Bellissima! One more time with the ball, but can you leap and attempt to kick a goal? We'll put some gym mats under you to soften your fall. Are you comfortable with that?'

'I'll do my best. Fire away.' It had dawned on me that I was probably shocking Enzo with my ability. But right then, I didn't care.

'Just one more thing, if you can, please make sure the ball is kicked either side of me. I don't fancy getting hit by a football and my camera won't enjoy it either.' Enzo looked genuinely concerned.

'Very funny, Enzo. I'll do my best but I can't guarantee that I won't hit you. Are you insured?'

'Yes, but I'm sure your kicks won't be too damaging. My assistant will throw the ball very gently at first and we'll see how you go.'

'I'm ready. Let's go,' I said. I couldn't wait to blast the balls past him.

At first I sent them back gently to warm up.

'Yes, I love that, Lucia. You have great skill,' said Enzo, still surprised.

Then I unleashed at full pace . . . bang, bang, bang, the balls flew past Enzo on both sides. Just for a bit of fun I sent a few balls flying just over his head. 'Hey, Lucia take it easy! But, this *is* fantastic. What else can you show me?' he said. I asked the assistant to throw the ball higher and I surprised him with a scissor kick.

Click, click, click. Enzo couldn't get enough. 'Spectacular, Lucia. You have the gift,' he cried with amazement, even though he had to duck a few times. 'Wait, Lucia's sweating,' Anastasia yelled out, stopping play. 'She needs powder and a few adjustments.'

Of course. Everything had to be perfect, I couldn't *possibly* have a hair out of place. Anastasia was like a demon with the hairspray, and carefully touched up my make-up.

'Lucia, keep still, I need to top up your lippy. Perfect, now you look like a model . . . or maybe a glamorous footballer! I had no idea you were so gifted with the ball. I'm so impressed.'

I smiled as she worked the big powder puff over my face.

'I've never seen you so excited at a photo session', she continued. 'I can't wait for your papa to see you perform your magic in front of the camera. Your parents must be so proud that the football genes have been passed on to you. What do they think of the way you play?'

I whispered, 'They don't know. I train secretly with my friends. Please, we must keep this between us.'

'You know I wouldn't say anything . . . but they'll see the photos,' said Anastasia.

She was right. What was I doing? I couldn't let Papa see me perform so competently with the ball. I was so much sharper and stronger than when I was banned from playing – he'd be able to see that I'd been practising behind his back. I tried to think of a way out, but before I could say anything to Enzo, Papa walked back into the studio.

'Sorry about that – I had to take that call.' He grimaced. 'How's it all going?'

'How's it going? This has to be one of the most incredible shoots I've ever worked on,' Enzo gushed. 'Lucia was born to play. Paolo, you must be so proud of her. You've taught her well.'

I cringed and waited for Papa's response.

'Enzo, I think the heat from the lights has burnt your brain. What are you talking about? Lucia doesn't play football any more. She's a model and a dancer, not a footballer,' Papa replied earnestly.

They looked at me. Sweat dripped down my face as nerves took over. This moment could change my life.

'Oh Lucia, show your papa how you can dance with the football. Show him how you juggle, and your spectacular scissor kicks. Paolo, she's like a prima ballerina, except she performs with a football – an absolute vision,' Enzo enthused.

Anastasia was back with the powder puff as I prepared for damage control. I gave her a wink and hoped for the best. This was going to be tough but I had to protect myself. Sorry, Enzo, I thought.

He threw me a ball and I clumsily fumbled around with it at my feet, tripping over and falling on the mat. I demonstrated very bad timing and a total lack of co-ordination.

Papa was convinced. 'See, Lucia's no footballer. Enzo, you must be overworked. You need to take a break.'

'No Paolo, I'm fine. I've never been better. I'm telling you, your daughter controls the football better than most people. She's just messing,' Enzo said firmly. Then he looked at me. 'Come on, Lucia, you're making me look like a fool. I'm going to show your papa the images I just shot, and he'll see your skills for himself. You should be proud of your ability. You're so talented. Why hide it?' He responded in disbelief.

I thought flattery would be my best defence. 'Enzo, I'm not hiding anything. You just know how to make me look good, that's why you're the best photographer in Italy.'

# Chapter 15

# Defy gravity

From: lucyzeezou@footballmail.com  To: bellabella@glamourmail.com
Subject: Ciao!

Hey Bella

How r u? Sorry I haven't been in contact sooner but it's been hectic back home.

I didn't realise how much I missed Milan, it's all so familiar and comfortable for me here. I met up with a few of my old football friends for a game in the park. It was fun catching up and hanging out, eating gelato and of course talking about my favourite subject. I've slipped back into my Italian lifestyle but I really miss you, the Lions and my grandparents.

I'm torn between the two cities, but I love the way Sydney gives us more freedom to do as we please. The paparazzi here won't leave us alone, it's suffocating.

I know you'll love this bit of news. I've just finished the Love Lucy photoshoot for my parents' new teen label and it was actually fun – although I nearly blew my secret. The outfits are quite sporty and casual, so the shoot had a sporty theme, and I ended up playing with a football. I think I may have got away with it for now, but it's going to be hard to explain how I juggled the ball so many times and managed scissor kicks. Papa will know that I've been training when he sees the shots. I smell trouble, but it was the best photoshoot I've ever been involved in. It won't be long before I have to face the music. There goes my football career, up in a puff of smoke . . . but I won't bore you with my stuff any more.

Gigi's keeping me occupied. I'm bringing her back with me – so you'll get to meet her soon. And the best news is that my papa may also be coming back with us.

How are the boys? Have you seen Harry or Max? What's the latest goss?

Say hi to Dylan. Sorry, have to go. Ciao

Lucy

'Lucy, I have something to show you. Can you please come up to the office?' Papa buzzed over the intercom.

'Okay, Papa, I'm on my way,' I replied. It wasn't often that he called me upstairs, so I wondered what was up.

The home office for 23 took up the whole fourth floor of our house, and it had spectacular views of the city. Wall-to-wall cabinets were crammed full of Papa's awards, trophies and memorabilia from his football career. While football dominated the space, Mama had managed to throw in a splash of fashion items to demonstrate that this was actually where my parents ran their fashion business.

The office was a recent addition, so that they could spend more time with me, although it hadn't worked out as well as I'd hoped. They still worked crazy hours, but at least now they were only a few levels above me.

As I approached the office door, I could hear voices. I'd thought Papa was alone, but I walked in on a business meeting. Mama was there, dressed as usual in her finest. 'My beautiful girl. Come in. Your mama and I have something we'd like to show you,' Papa said with a look of delight while Mama gave me a curious stare.

This wasn't good.

'What is it, Papa?' I said, trying to sound enthusiastic.

My stomach was in knots.

'Enzo has brought over the proofs from yesterday's shoot. We want to see what you think of them,' he said enthusiastically.

'Oh, but I don't usually like to look at them. I'm sure you'll choose the best shot for the campaign,' I replied anxiously.

'Don't be so modest. I want you to take a good look and select your favourite. Enzo here tells me they're very impressive. Oh, and this is our friend Marcello Lantini. He's a filmmaker.'

'Ciao, Enzo. Nice to meet you Signor Lantini.'

'Please call me Marcello,' he said, inspecting me closely. I didn't like it, but I was pretty much used to it. I stared straight back at him and he averted his eyes.

I sat at Papa's desk, expecting the shots to come up on his computer screen, but it was blank.

Suddenly the movie screen unfolded from the ceiling. The lights went out and music began to play. Next thing I knew, I was bombarded with images of myself from the Love Lucy fashion shoot. I could barely believe it.

All the shots with the football looked amazing. Now I was really panicking. I had the distinct feeling that my relationship with football would soon be a distant memory.

Despite my nerves, I could see that the photos were very impressive. I looked over at Enzo, who gave me a quick wink. A sheepish smile sprawled across his face. My parents hadn't taken their eyes off the screen; they were scrutinising every shot. Papa seemed impressed, but it was hard to tell, as he didn't utter a word. Mama, however, looked horrified. Her face turned red as the football shots filled the screen and mesmerised the small audience.

I shrank into my seat, wondering how I'd explain my football skills. I prayed for the time to go quickly, wishing it was just a bad dream, some awful mistake. But then the lights went on and when I looked up, all four of them were staring at me, astonished.

'Lucia, that was simply stunning. Your magic in front of the camera has given us so much to choose from. This campaign will cause a sensation when it's released. The mix of your modelling and football skills is incredible – mind-boggling. Italy, in fact Europe, will fall in love with Lucy!' Enzo could barely contain his excitement.

Mama was unusually quiet. Papa, who still looked amazed, spoke instead. 'Lucia . . . words can't express how I feel. The image you portray is full of life, elegance and confidence. I'm surprised, pleased and also confused: I don't know how or where you managed to learn to use the football in such a masterful way when you don't play anymore.

I sank further into my seat, anticipating a lecture. 'Your beloved Nonno Dino obviously left a lasting impression. When I saw you at the shoot you were falling over the football. But on the screen, you defy gravity . . . it's mesmerising. I don't want answers right now – in fact, I've just thought of a good tagline for the television campaign: "Defy gravity . . . in Love Lucy designs". '

*A television campaign?* Oh no. This was getting out of control. I had to do something.

'Yes, that's a great idea. I love it,' said Enzo with an enormous grin.

'"Defy gravity in Love Lucy designs" – it defines the label and it's something that young people will find appealing. Lucia is perfect, she already portrays that image. Brilliant!' agreed Marcello.

'Frida you've been very quiet. What do you think?' asked Papa.

'Well, I'm shocked, but I confess I'm in awe of Lucy's performance as a model. The images are stunning, and I actually like the fashion and sport mix.'

Oooh, that was a big surprise.

Mama continued. 'In this case it works. The camera loves her and here she is in love with the camera and, it seems, the football. She'll certainly demand attention; Girls will want to be like her and boys will wonder how she does it.'

By this stage I was cowering in my chair. I was in deep trouble. There was no way Mama would let me get away with this.

'Unlike you, Paolo, I *would* like to know how she demonstrates such mastery with the ball – or is it just Enzo's incredible talent with the camera? If you remember, we stopped her playing last year, but I can't recall seeing her leap in the air like that back then. I hope she's dancing with the same dedication she seems to have given football – but I'll discuss that with her later, as it's a personal matter.' Mama crossed her arms and gave me one of her looks.

'Great, it's settled,' said Papa.

But Mama wasn't finished. 'Oh and one more thing – Enzo, I congratulate you for doing such an amazing job – it's your best work. You've captured a Lucia I didn't know, and I love it. It's a look and mood that I know will be popular. Translated into a television commercial, this will certainly be a success.'

'Well, that's settled, then,' said Papa. 'We'll film the commercial in three weeks, Lucia, so make sure you get plenty of rest so that you look your best – and please stay off your bicycle. We don't want any injuries or bruises.'

My stomach was churning and my temper rising. I was overcome with emotion and couldn't stop myself . . . 'I thought you wanted my opinion. I thought we were going back to Sydney in two weeks. I have other important commitments, like school and my dance concert. I have another life with Grandpa and Nanna in Australia, and I miss my new friends. I can't just hang around while you plot and plan my future. I've had it,' I cried.

Everyone looked at me, stunned. I stormed out of the room.

# Chapter 16

# Figlia d'arte

I couldn't take it any more. My life was spinning out of control. I locked myself in my bedroom and wept.

'Lucia? Open the door this instant,' yelled Mama. 'My beautiful girl, come on, let Papa in. We must talk,' he pleaded.

I ignored them. My own parents didn't know me. How could they be so blind? They only saw what they wanted to see. If they bothered to look at me or listen to me they'd find a completely different person longing to be understood.

I lay on the bed, staring at the ceiling and trying to work out how I was going to get out of this one. I had to get back for the Champion of Champions tournament. I didn't want to let my team down.

I drifted off to sleep, slipping into a dream where I was playing with my hero Zinedine Zidane again. This time, I was ready to take the penalty. He said, 'I know you can do it. I know you can do it.' I struck the penalty with confidence and watched the ball float in the air towards my target, but I was disturbed by loud banging. I opened my eyes and thought about what my hero had said, but the banging didn't stop.

'Lucia, um, Lucy, you must open the door so that we can discuss this. We need to work it out. Come on, please open the door,' Papa appealed.

I'd have to face the drama sooner or later. I slowly rose and opened the door, and fell into Papa's arms.

'My Lucia, why are you so sad? We just want the best for you. You must know we love you more than anything? I thought you'd be honoured to be the face of our campaign.'

I could hear the concern in his voice. I knew he loved me, but he just didn't get me. Maybe that's what it was like with all kids. Were we all misunderstood?

'Papa, I'm confused. I thought we were going back to Australia in two weeks. I've made lots of friends and have commitments there. And you know what, I really love it in Sydney because we're left alone by the paparazzi. We have space to be who we want to be, like any normal family.' Papa gently stroked my head as I spoke. 'I'm very happy to be a part of your campaign, but I'm scared of being famous. Look what it's like for you, walking down the street is a nightmare.'

'My sweet Lucia, fame is something you've grown up with. You are a *figlia d'arte* – the child of an accomplished famous person. This is your destiny.'

Great, can't beat destiny, I thought wryly.

'I can't change that. I didn't realise you felt so strongly about it. But look at the positive side . . . you can use your position to make a difference in the world. You have the chance to help others. I know it can be very testing, being pursued by the photographers. But in the end, we have a life where we can basically do as we please. How about I talk to Mama and we can look into filming the commercial in Sydney, so that you can get back in time for school and your concert as planned. Does that sound better?'

'Thank you, Papa. That means a lot to me,' I replied, feeling a bit calmer.

'Lucia, you mean everything to me. All I want is your happiness.'

But the one thing that would make me happy was something he disapproved of. I couldn't ask again, not yet.

'Thanks Papa. I feel better, and one thing that would make me even happier is for you to call me Lucy.'

'Of course, Lucy . . . I love Lucy!'

From: bellabella@glamourmail.com  To: lucyzeezou@footballmail. com Subject: RE: Ciao!

Hey Lucy

It sounds like you're having a ball in Milan. Please send me some photos if you have time. I've never been to Italy and I'd love to go . . . one of these days. And I'd like to check out your friends!

Tell me more about the photoshoot – you lucky thing. I'm so jealous. I'd give my right arm to be in a professional shoot and have my hair and make-up done . . . someone fussing over me all day . . . what a dream! I don't suppose they'd like a bookworm with glasses and braces instead?

Anyway, fill me in on every detail. What are the clothes like? Is the photographer cute? How did the shots turn out? And what do you mean you nearly blew your secret?

What happened?

I can't say I've been doing much with my holidays. Nothing has changed except that some of the cool girls are now talking to me, even that bully Claudia, and it's all because of you. I ran into one of them and accidentally told her about your Love Lucy fashion shoot . . . I couldn't help myself . . . I was so excited I had to tell someone and the next thing I know the news had spread. Most of them think what you're doing is really cool, even though they're jealous. Sorry!

Yes, Harry's been hanging out at the Reg kicking the ball with Dylan in between training sessions with the Lions. You know I don't like him – he's a jock, so I have nothing to say to him. He just talks about football and always asks after you. Can you please drop him a line? He's unbearable.

No one's heard from Max – he seems to have disappeared. Dylan asked your grandpa about him and he hasn't heard anything either. I'm sure he's okay, although Harry's ready to take another swipe at him. He's probably sulking at home, wherever that is. No need to worry.

Dylan says hi and wants me to tell you that they've been winning and have reached the quarter-finals of the Champion of Champions. So you should be back in time for the final, if they keep winning. They're looking forward to having you back on the pitch. Now there's a turn for the books! They've finally woken up to the fact that girls can be as good as boys – well, it should be better, in your case. Or is it that absence makes the heart grow fonder? I think my bro likes you.

Anyway, I miss you and can't wait to see you back in Oz.

Luv Bella

From: lucyzeezou@footballmail.com  To: bellabella@glamourmail.com Subject: RE: RE: Ciao!

Hey Bella

Great to hear from you.

I'm so thrilled the boys have reached the quarter-finals but I'm really worried about Max. Someone has to know where he is. You've got to find out more.

I need to tell you something in confidence and please don't even tell Dylan: Max doesn't have a home. He's a street kid and has been living in the stands at the Reg. We've got to help him. Please find out whatever you can about his whereabouts and get back to me ASAP.

My parents almost finding out that I play football is now the least of my problems. I've just been told that we may be staying another couple of weeks so that I can be the face of a television commercial for the Love Lucy label. So right now I'm not very happy. I don't want to let the boys down. I want to be back for the final.

Papa said that they may shoot the ad in Sydney after I chucked a hissy fit, but who knows if Mama will allow it. I'll let you know what the verdict is soon. Fingers crossed.

Please don't tell the boys yet, I don't want to end up in their bad books yet again. And all is forgiven about letting it slip re the fashion shoot but please . . . no more blabbing about me to the girls from school, they're just going to tease me no matter what I do.

Oh and by the way, of course you could model. Don't let glasses and braces stop you. You can hang out on set with me if we shoot the commercial in Sydney and then you'll see it's not as glamorous as you think.

Let's trade places. Ciao

Lucy

I was interrupted by a knock at my door. 'Who is it?'

'It's Mama. Lucia, can you please open the door? I've brought you some snacks and a hot chocolate,' she said softly.

She knew how to get to me. We may have had our differences but Mama and I had one major thing in common . . . we *loved* our food.

I welcomed her in.

We gave each other a tentative smile, then hugged. 'Lucy, I wish I could understand what's going on in

your head. We only want the best for you and we've been through this before. Most girls can only ever dream about an opportunity like this! I wish I'd had these chances when I was your age.' Mama put on her businesslike voice again. 'Anyway, you can act the drama queen all you like but, you've got to do the commercial and there's no getting out of it.'

'Calm down, Mama, I'm doing it. I can't wait,' I tried to inject some enthusiasm into my voice.

'You may be able to fool Papa but there's no need to be sarcastic. And how did you come up with those kicks at the shoot when you were forbidden to play over a year ago?'

'Oh, Mama, I remember everything Nonno Dino taught me. I'll never forget him and his football stories. We used to practise those kicks all day, every day. Really, it's no big deal.' I tried to sound cool.

What I just said was almost true – I wasn't really lying, I just left out a few minor details. But what they didn't know wouldn't hurt them.

'Okay, Lucy, I'll accept that answer for now, only because it works for the campaign and we've been through enough today. All I ask is that you perform at your best for the commercial. No more questions . . . for now!'

What a relief!

'Okay, Mama. I'll do my best. But . . . are we going to film it in Australia?'

'Well, I know you have to get back for your dance concert, and for school. I love the fact that you're so committed to them, so we're trying to work it out with Marcello and Enzo, as we want them both working on it.'

'Oh thanks, Mama. And yes, the concert is very important. We've worked so hard to get it right, I'd hate to miss it. You're the best.'

Okay, so I told an even bigger fib. I couldn't get out of that one. Luckily I'd scraped in a few dance classes so it shouldn't be too difficult catching up when I returned. It'd be a doddle . . . wouldn't it?

# Chapter 17

# Finding Max

From: bellabella@glamourmail.com  To: lucyzeezou@footballmail.com
Subject: Max missing

Hi Lucy

How's Milan treating you?

Good news. The boys have made it to the final of the Champion of Champions. Do you think you'll be back in time? Coach James wants to know if you'll be available. I think they're getting worried!

Sorry, it wasn't me who told him you may still be away. Dylan snuck in and read the last email you sent me and blabbed. We had a big fight over it. He's also upset because he thinks you don't care about the competition, and he's wondering who your Italian football friends are. Now I'm pretty sure that he has a crush on you. He's also shocked about the news I'm about to share with you.

I don't know how to say this, but Max is in a lot of trouble and he could be in danger. No one can find him and now the police are looking for him.

Apparently Max was caught up in a fight at Rushcutters Bay Park with a gang of boys. He managed to get out of there before the police arrived, but the awful thing is that he hit a guy (in self-defence, everyone says) who ended up in hospital. So someone reported him to the police for that, and now they're looking for him. And to make matters worse, they've realised that he's the same boy who ran away from his foster parents about a year ago. It's been reported in the news – what a mess.

They found Max's backpack and football boots at the edge of a mooring near the yacht club. The worst thing is, they discovered blood along the wharf. He may be hurt.

The police have put up missing signs all around the Cross and surrounding neighbourhoods. They've searched the whole area and have had divers in the harbour searching for clues. It's all very scary and it's weird seeing his photo out in public like that.

Everyone's really worried about him, including Harry. Now he feels bad about the fight they had and he feels even worse that he didn't know that Max was homeless. He would have done more to help him. We're all in shock and trying to help find him.

I'm sorry that the news isn't good but I had to tell you. Take care

Luv Bella

From: lucyzeezou@footballmail.com To: bellabella@glamourmail. com Subject: Oh no!

OMG, Bella!

I can't believe it! How did all of this happen? Poor Max. I feel so useless being so far away. What if he's badly hurt? It's so awful thinking what might have happened to him, and the fact that he's got no one to turn to.

The time here is going quickly but not fast enough now that I know about Max's situation. I just want to come back and help find him.

Please tell Coach James that I'm going to make sure that I'm back for the final. I can't wait to get onto the pitch . . . life's much easier when you're just chasing a ball.

My parents have just agreed to film the commercial in Sydney, even though it's probably going to cost them more money. But I really don't care about anything like that at the moment, I'm more concerned about Max.

Please call me as soon as you hear anything.

I'm going to watch my papa play in the big local derby this Sunday. I've been looking forward to this game since we arrived. Papa said I can hang out with him after the game . . . At least that will help take my mind off Max for a bit. It's something to look forward to.

Oh and about Dylan. He's my friend and that's it. I'm not interested in anyone that way.

Please contact me ASAP if you hear any more news about Max.

Luv Lucy

I couldn't believe what was going on in my life. One minute everything was fine and the next it was all upside down.

How could we find Max? Maybe I could ask Papa to hire a private investigator to find him or Bella could ask her mama; surely she'd have all the right connections. Someone had to know something.

At least I'd be back in Sydney in time for the final. Everything was straightforward on the pitch. You worked with your team mates against the opposition. It was so simple. Why couldn't life be like that?

What was I going to do about Dylan? It was such an awkward situation. We were just friends and that was it. I'd just have to try and act cool around him. I didn't want to hurt his feelings, but I just didn't like anyone that way. At least, I didn't think so . . .

# Chapter 18

# The derby

Mama and I were finally off to the derby. All morning I was jumping out of my skin to get there, worried that we wouldn't arrive in time for kick-off, since Mama was fussing over her outfit. Papa was at his team's base, Milanello, preparing for the game and would arrive at the San Siro with his team mates and AC Milan staff. Papa didn't really get that nervous before a game, but he *was* superstitious. I wasn't supposed to know it, but he wouldn't walk onto that pitch unless he was wearing his lucky red undies!

The derby was one of the biggest games on the world football calendar – a clash between two local rivals, AC Milan and Inter Milan. The city was buzzing with anticipation, and divided into a sea of AC Milan's red and black colours and Inter's blue and black. Everyone supported one of the clubs, or if not they'd at least have an opinion of the encounter. Even though the game was played on Sunday, most people would skip church and tune into the radio or TV to watch it if they couldn't get tickets. And then they'd spend most of Monday conducting post mortems on the game. It was intoxicating, and I loved it! The match today was a particularly special one, because the clubs were promoting football against racism. It was a global campaign run by football's governing body, aiming to encourage inclusiveness and stamp out racism. That was something I loved about football – it had the power to break social and racial barriers and raise awareness. Players came from all parts of the world and they were usually embraced by their team mates and supporters. Even my team in Sydney had players from eleven different backgrounds, out of a squad of sixteen.

But there were still some narrow-minded fans who were prejudiced against a particular race or religion.

I didn't understand how people could not see the benefits of being part of a planet full of different cultures. It would be so boring if we were all the same.

While the players fought for points on the pitch, another war was looming in the players' box, where the footballers' friends and family sat. Mama and the other wives and hangers on all tried to outdo each other in the latest fashions, sipping only the best champagne. It was nearly as competitive as the football, which they didn't really care about – although they cheered on cue, vying to attract the cameras.

The kids were okay . . . at least they showed more interest in the game, except for the other girls my age and a bit older who were far too girly for my liking.

We settled ourselves in the box, and Mama turned to me. 'Lucia, could you at least put on a little bit of lipstick? You look a little dishevelled, honey, and the cameras are bound to look for us at some point.' She handed me a new hot-pink lipstick. I threw it in my pocket while she wasn't looking.

I decided to escape the irritating fashion scene for my own sanity, hoping to catch up with Papa and his team mates before kick-off, and then watch the match from the stands.

'Mama, I'll be back soon, I'm just going to catch up with an old friend I can see in the stands.'

'Why don't you tell her to come up? You don't want to watch the game from down there.' I swear I could see Mama's nose turn up at the thought of me sitting with the rest of the fans. I rolled my eyes. Mama really did live on another planet. I wanted to watch the game with the real fans who understood football.

'It's okay, Mama . . . Don't worry, I'll be back soon.' I planted a kiss on both cheeks and was off.

Another lie. Well, it was a small one.

I ran down into the belly of the stadium towards the tunnel, which I could enter only because I had a special access-all-areas pass. I hoped I wasn't too late to catch Papa before he ran onto the pitch. I loved seeing the players just before they headed out. You could really feel the tension and excitement before a big clash.

While they waited in the tunnel, each player stood with a child, who they'd lead out onto the pitch. Being a mascot was something kids dreamt of. I used to run out with Papa when I was little, for special occasions like his hundredth game for the club and big final match days, but now I was too old for that.

I caught Papa and his team a few moments before he was to lead them out. I said hello to the players. Some were wriggling out their nerves, while the older, more experienced players were chilled, like my papa. The opposition stood nearby, adding to the tension.

I wrapped myself around Papa and whispered, 'Good luck, Papa. Score a goal for me.'

He answered with a tighter bear hug. 'I'll do my best, but you know my job is to defend. If I get a chance, I'll crack the ball into the back of the net, especially for you. I'll celebrate by blowing you a kiss.'

It was true that he rarely scored goals, but I sensed that today would be different. He led the team out with a look of determination. I watched, dreaming that one day I'd lead my own team out into this arena.

I stayed to watch the game from down there, within view of the bench and coach. He was yelling instructions from the sidelines as the players fought for the ball. I could smell the manicured grass and hear the clash of boots. There was nothing like being in the San Siro on derby day, surrounded by the roar of the crowd. They chanted their team songs and madly waved their flags. It was impossible not to be swept up in the excitement and passion of the die-hard fans.

And seeing Papa play made my spine tingle. Straight from kick-off he was involved, directing and encouraging his players. He guarded the back line like his life depended on it, so it was extremely tough for the opposition to get past him. He read the play very early, which gave him an edge over his rivals. That's why he was considered one of the best.

The crowd went wild as AC Milan created the first shots on goal and Papa put himself in contention. Inter's goalkeeper staved off the attempts and the ball was sent back to the halfway mark. But moments later, Inter managed to silence the *rossoneri*, AC Milan's fans, with an unexpected opening goal that seemed to come from nowhere. The stadium was dominated by chants from the *nerazzurri*, Inter's supporters, but not for long. Three minutes later, Kaká worked his magic from the halfway line and beat the keeper with a spectacular goal to level the match. The Inter fans fell silent as the air was saturated with AC Milan's supporters in full voice and of course I joined in the celebrations.

Soon it was close to half-time, and I thought I should go back and find Mama, in case she was worried.

I started to head back up the stairs to the players' box, still daydreaming about being a professional and playing in front of fanatical supporters. I was suddenly struck by the sound of heavy breathing behind me . . . before I could turn to see who it was, a hand squeezed over my mouth. I struggled to scream, but the grip was too tight. The next thing I knew, I was being carried away up flights of stairs.

I tried to kick my way free but the person was too strong. I must have lost consciousness, because next thing I knew, I was waking to the sound of distant cheering. I didn't know how long I'd been out. I opened my eyes to inspect my surroundings, and realised that there was tape over my mouth and my arms were tied behind my back. Oh no! My heart pounded heavily in my chest.

What was going on? Was this some sort of sick joke? My thoughts raced and beads of sweat trickled down my face in the stifling, windowless room. I was being held hostage, somewhere in the stadium.

Across the room I spotted a man and a woman dressed all in black, with dark wrap-around sunnies and peaked caps. They were deep in conversation, speaking in a foreign language.

The sound of my backpack vibrating on the ground interrupted them. It was probably Mama ringing, wondering where I was. They stared at the backpack, panic-stricken. This was not part of their plan. The woman reached down and tipped everything out of the bag. To my surprise, she answered the phone.

Her accomplice yelled something. I couldn't understand the words, but judging by his expression and tone of voice, he was saying, 'No, DON'T!'

While they were distracted, I tried to struggle free, but it was no use – the tape, or whatever was binding my hands, was too tight. The man noticed my desperate efforts and launched towards me.

'Don't try anythink or you dead,' he snarled in a heavy accent, standing over me like a big thug.

Now I was really scared . . . terrified. I sat perfectly still and did my best to listen to the phone call. The woman's English was so bad it was hard to understand her. She said 'Lucia not come bark!' into the phone and then switched it off.

The man yelled at her frantically, his face consumed with anger. I wished I could tell what they were saying. She yelled back at him, gestured with her arms and pointed at me and the door.

The man then lifted his shirt. To my horror, a gun rested on his hip. He looked like a hit man – those scary fit ones that you saw in Hollywood movies. I wished I was in a movie and not living this nightmare.

How had he slipped past security with a gun?

This was not a person to mess with. Someone had to help me . . . surely Mama would have called the police by now? I'd been missing for most of the game – but then again, I told her I'd be with a friend. Maybe she thought I was hanging out with her until the game was over. My little lie had backfired – and it might be my last.

# Chapter 19

# The kiss

I tried to pulled myself together, focusing on the sounds that filled the room. I could hear the fans cheering. Suddenly, the cheers mellowed and I could make out the match commentary in the background.

That was it! I was being held next to the commentary box!

'AC Milan and Inter have locked horns . . . this game is panning out to be yet another classic . . .'

But the commentary was bluntly interrupted by the woman yelling instructions. 'Look this way, Lucia. HEY! I say look this way or you be sorry.'

I turned and saw that she was fiddling with a camera. I was frightened, hot and extremely angry, sitting on the concrete floor without any idea why I had been kidnapped. And now they wanted to take my photo, of all the weird things. Why?

This was infuriating – I couldn't even get away from the camera as a hostage. I reluctantly followed her orders and stared into the camera.

She took the photo and made a quick exit, leaving me with the big scary man. I was shaking, and began to sob uncontrollably. He walked over to me. 'Why you cry?'

What kind of stupid question was that? Now I knew what I was dealing with. I struggled to speak through the tape and, unexpectedly, he ripped it off my mouth.

'Ouch that hurt!' And then I pleaded, 'Please, let me go . . . please! I just want to be with my family. I want to go home.'

He took off his cap and sunglasses and crouched next to me. I was surprised by how young he looked. But he dashed my hopes. 'Impossible.'

'Why can't you let me go? Why have I been abducted?' I asked, trying to control my tears.

'You . . . held for ransom. Your father get letter to give us millions of US dollars, which must deliver by tomorrow afternoon . . . then you go.' His accent was just as strong as the woman's.

'How could you do this? You seem too young to carry a gun and commit a serious crime. You'll go to jail. How old *are* you?' I queried, hoping to appeal to his soft side – if there was one. I thought if I managed to strike up a conversation and sound interested in him he might let me go.

'I'm seventeen. I'm fighting for my brothers. They have no jobs, no money . . . nothing. Every day struggle with no hope. But you have everything because you very rich.'

'But you'll just get into trouble. Please let me go, and I'll make sure you can get away,' I begged him.

'No! You my prisoner. My people very poor, they need my help,' he replied, as though reading lines from a very bad movie.

And then, bizarrely, he lunged down and attempted to steal a kiss. I was completely astonished but reacted aggressively, biting him hard on the lips. He pulled back and moaned, holding his mouth. Instinctively, I kicked him in the groin as though I was striking the football into the goal. He crouched down in pain, and I made a run for the door. I couldn't open it because my hands were tightly bound. I banged the door with my head, as if attempting a header in a game . . . this time it really was the game of life and I screamed my head off. But the crowd had resumed chanting, and I was drowned out.

As the weirdo attempted to grab me, the door swung open, smacking me on the nose. I yelled in pain. His accomplice stormed in from her brief mission and pushed me to the ground, yelling something I couldn't understand.

I turned to see the young guy's lip bleeding. He was pointing his gun in my direction. I was still shaking, and now blood was pouring from my nose. The sight of it added to my terror, but strangely it also gave me a push to fight back.

'You won't get away with this,' I said loudly.

The woman grabbed me by the hair. 'We already have.' She looked at the man. 'Give her tissue and tape her mouth up . . . now!'

# Chapter 20

# Lipstick

The game came to an end at last. I could hear cheering and booing fill the stadium. The fans would be starting to leave. The victors continued to sing their team song and it was the familiar sound of the AC Milan chant. At least one good thing had come out of today . . . Papa's team had won.

I strained to hear the commentators. 'Let's take a look at the highlights. Inter snatched the lead in the opening five minutes but their glory was short-lived. Goals by Kaká and Inzaghi gave Milan a 2–1 lead at the break. Inter fought back late in the second half to equalise and then the brilliant Paolo Zoffi took everyone in his path by surprise, attacking and running up the pitch until he reached the 18-yard box. A few seconds from full-time, with the score locked at 2–2, he took an unexpected shot on goal . . . the crowd was stunned into silence. The ball found its target, giving Milan a dramatic 3–2 victory.'

Papa had scored! Even though I was terrified about my predicament, I felt a thrill of victory.

I listened to more of the commentary: 'Sensational scenes followed and the fans went into hysterics. The famous number 23 is celebrating by lifting his jersey to reveal a black singlet with a large red heart. Ah yes, it has his daughter Lucy's name and the words "Defy Gravity" across the back. The captain knows how to work the crowd and they are *loving* it. He's blowing kisses to them and the players' box. The *rossoneri* are filling the stadium with their hero's famous name: ZOFFI, ZOFFI, ZOFFI!'

He was my hero, too, and that spectacular win inspired me, giving me extra incentive to take control. I had to act now, as the commentators would be leaving shortly for the press conference and interviews with players and managers. I had an idea. I squatted as though I was on the toilet. They looked at me like I was crazy. The woman ripped off my tape. 'What you doing?'

'Please, I have to go to the bathroom urgently,' I pleaded.

'You hold on,' the woman shrieked. 'Shut her mouth up,' she ordered.

'Wait! Please . . . I can't . . . I have to poo,' I claimed.

How embarrassing.

'Ahh. Okay. I take you, but if you try to run or scream, you'll be very, very sorry,' she said as she flashed her gun at me.

She put a jacket over my shoulders and hooked her arm tightly around mine. We moved past unsuspecting fans as they celebrated AC Milan's victory. The commentary box and television studio was to my left. I'd been there many times before with Papa. The windows faced the pitch, so we couldn't be seen as we walked past.

She took me down the corridor and made a sharp left turn to the toilets. I knew this area well . . . all I needed now was to get loose.

Surprisingly, the toilets were vacant. The woman poked the gun into my back and commanded, 'Don't be long.'

'I can't go to the toilet with my hands tied,' I urged, still terrified.

She looked at me with darting eyes, pulled out a knife and cut me loose. 'Okay, but don't try anything. I use my gun if you try and escape.'

I nervously nodded, but I knew that this was my only chance. I locked the door behind me and tried to think of a way out.

'Hurry! If you not out in two minutes, I come get you,' she said. I could see the backs of her dirty men's boots under the door.

She fell silent and relaxed her stance when a couple of fans entered the toilets, talking about the game. Their presence gave me hope. I looked under the partition and noticed that one of them was in the cubicle next to me.

It was now or never. I searched through my pockets and found the pink lipstick Mama had given me earlier. Luckily it was hot-pink – not my colour, but bright enough to be useful now. On a bit of toilet paper I quickly scribbled:

*HELP! Woman at door has gun!*

*I'm being held hostage next to media box. This is not a joke. Please get help.*

*Lucia Zoffi No. 23*

So, there was a use for lipstick after all – today I was grateful for girly stuff . . . thank you, Mama! I wrapped the note around the lipstick and passed it under the toilet partition, hoping the fan would grab it. She did. I breathed a sigh of relief. Now I could only hope that she would raise the alarm and not just keep the lippy.

I focused on my next move as I heard her open her door. She didn't even wash her hands. It sounded as though she whisked her friend away quickly. Now I had to act before my captor became suspicious. She was still standing in front of my cubicle's door.

'Okay, enough. I come in,' she said impatiently. 'Please, I'm just wiping my bottom,' I lied frantically.

I closed my eyes and pretended I was on the football pitch, prowling in front of the goal. I imagined booting the ball into the back of the net . . . I struck and the door miraculously came tumbling down, knocking her to the ground. Although my foot was killing me, I jumped over her and ran for my life. She screamed, 'Stop or I shoot!' But I didn't care. I took a risk and kept running as she fired.

# Chapter 21

# The ransom

The team would celebrate with a victory lap, thanking their fans for their unwavering support.

The crowd would continue to applaud their heroes with more chanting, singing and cheering which reverberates throughout the iconic stadium.

Then the players would disappear into the tunnel, heading to their change rooms for a well-deserved rest. A massage and ice bath awaited them.

I knew the drill. The press conference would be starting right now.

Papa and the coach would face a packed media conference. As captain, Papa would encounter a barrage of questions about the spectacular win and his unexpected goal.

From my vantage point – crouched in an alcove and half-hidden by a row of seats – I had a good view of the big screen at one end of the stadium. The press conference was being beamed out to a live television audience. The crowd of journalists, hungry for a story, started yelling out their questions.

'Paolo, how does it feel for a world class defender to score the winning goal?'

Papa didn't get a chance to answer. The club's president barged in, surrounded by a throng of bodyguards. The room was abuzz.

'Apologies everyone,' he said in a sombre tone, 'but Paolo Zoffi is needed for a pressing matter. He won't be taking any further questions. His team mates and fellow goal-scorers Kaká and Inzaghi are more than happy to oblige. Thank you.'

The gallery erupted as interest switched to Papa's sensational departure, and more pressing questions exploded from the confused media.

'This is unprecedented, what could be so pressing?' 'But what is this urgent matter?'

'Is there a problem with the players?'

It was a relief to know that someone must have been alerted to my abduction. Papa would make sure I was rescued, and in the meantime I had to work out a strategy to stay free and alive.

Then the screen dramatically went black, before showing a man wearing black clothes and a balaclava. This was bizarre! The image was being transmitted throughout the stadium on the big screens. They must have hacked their way into the system somehow. I could see fans frozen to the spot, just as I was in my little hideout.

The man made his demand slowly in accented tones. 'We are holding Paolo Zoffi's daughter Lucia captive.' There was something utterly chilling about the way he spoke and his presence on the screen. It was even more frightening when I realised this meant there was at least a third lunatic out to get me.

The man held up a photograph of me, the camera zooming in on my terrified, shocked face. A chill ripped along my spine as I watched. This must have been their back-up plan. The remaining fans still haven't moved, riveted to the spot as they witnessed the calculating delivery. I needed to get to safety, but I couldn't look away until he was finished.

'As you can see, we have your lovely Lucia. If you want to see your daughter alive you must organise a helicopter to take us to Malpensa airport, where we expect you to hand over twenty million US dollars in cash in exchange for your precious girl.' His tone became even more intense. 'Come alone, Signor Zoffi . . . if we see any police presence, you'll never see your daughter again.'

He ripped the photograph in half, while staring at the camera. 'You will receive further instructions when you arrive *alone* at the airport. You have three hours.'

And then the screen went blank.

They were bluffing . . . I wished I could tell Papa, I wished the police would find me. My legs were shaking as I contemplated the crazy situation. I was terrified, but my poor parents! They must have been going through hell.

I tried to pull myself together. I had to. Remember, I told myself, you're Lucy Zeezou. I'd escaped and they were *not* going to recapture me. I was the elusive striker, manoeuvring with precision and outwitting my rivals until I reached my goal.

# Chapter 22

# Adrenalin rush

The San Siro was in a state of pandemonium . . . fans were either frozen in their seats or running to collect their children and escape the horrible situation.

A voice over the loudspeaker called for order. 'Attention everyone . . . please remain calm. For your own safety you are advised to make your way to an exit turnstile. No one can leave the stadium until they have undertaken a police check. Please proceed with caution. Thank you for your cooperation.'

Amid the chaos, I carefully slipped out of my hiding spot, hoping to blend into the crowd but then the female abductor suddenly came into view. There were hundreds of shocked people between us, but that didn't make me feel safe. Where were the police?

I quickly made my way back to the media box in the hope someone would be there to help me, but it had been roped off. Two armed men dressed in some sort of dark combat gear with a red stripe stopped me.

One of them shouted, 'Signorina Zoffi . . . don't move.

We're part of the rescue squad.'

But I was terrified . . . I wasn't sure who I could trust, and I had to make a split-second decision as the woman with the gun was drawing nearer.

Then I heard a familiar voice among the madness. 'Lucia! It's Papa.' I turned and saw him at the top of the stairs, still in his football gear and surrounded by the police.

In that instant, my legs were taken from under me. 'Papa, help me,' I screamed as I was tackled to the ground by the other abductor, the young man who'd tried to kiss me. He dragged me to my feet and pushed something into my back. It must have been his gun. He bellowed, 'Nobody move or she gets it.'

'Please don't hurt her, take me instead. Please, you can have anything you want. Let her go,' called Papa, as the police held him back.

It was horrifying, unbelievable. The abductor had me in a tight grip, but I could feel that he was shaking nearly as much as I was.

He whispered in my ear, 'I am sorry, Lucia.'

But he didn't harm me. Instead, he fired at the police. Suddenly there was an eerie silence, promptly interrupted by the female abductor screeching like a wounded cat somewhere off to my side.

The man's grip loosened, and then he was no longer behind me.

I turned to see him slumped on the ground, with blood flowing from his leg. His face was blank with shock. I screamed once, like I've never screamed before, then I stared at him, feeling numb and terrified.

Someone shouted, 'Lucia, drop to the floor, now!'

Instinctively I took the orders as if my coach had yelled them from the sidelines.

I looked up and saw the woman now just a few metres away from me, still screaming, and with a gun in her hand. Before she could get any closer, the police pounced on her. They got into a tussle and she was subdued . . . she burst into tears.

I was completely exhausted. This had to be the worst experience of my life, almost surreal, like a scary movie. Papa ran over to me. He picked me up and cradled me like a baby.

'My beautiful girl, thank goodness you're okay. Did they hurt you?' he asked with tears in his eyes.

'No Papa, I'm just so tired. I want to go home.' I quivered.

'Let's get out of here. Mama is waiting for us in the president's office,' he said, his voice shaky.

'Signor Zoffi, your daughter must come with me to make a statement,' a policeman said.

'She is not going anywhere. She's been through a terrifying ordeal and needs to rest. You can see her when she's ready,' Papa argued, hugging me tighter and walking towards the office.

The policeman attempted to keep up, determined to have his way. 'But Signor Zoffi, we must find out what happened. A major crime has just been committed and we need answers. Signorina Zoffi must be examined,' he blustered.

'You need to examine security first and find out how these lunatics were able to enter the stadium with guns and abduct my daughter. Were they napping? Now leave us alone,' Papa fired back angrily.

The policeman stormed off.

Papa walked into the president's office and gently put me down, and Mama wrapped her arms around us. I was enveloped in one big, warm family embrace. I'm so lucky to have such loving parents . . . My thoughts shifted to Max. How awful not to have a loving family, people who really cared about you, especially at times like this. I started to cry again. I was more fortunate than I'd ever realised – I wouldn't trade this for the world.

'Lucia, thank goodness you're safe! We were so worried about you, my angel. Did they hurt you?' cried Mama.

I tried to pull myself together, although I was still trembling. 'I'm all right, Mama, I'm fine . . . really.' I wiped away my tears. 'I just want to go home. Oh and Papa, congratulations!'

They both looked at me. Papa asked, 'What do you mean, Lucia?'

'Your goal, Papa. I heard that you sealed the winner,' I said, forcing a smile.

'Lucy, you amaze me. I can't believe your bravery. It's not the time to be thinking about football.' He looked at me and laughed. 'How on earth did you manage to find out about the result while being held captive?'

'I could faintly hear the action from the commentary box, and I focused on it. It made me feel closer to you and it inspired me to escape. I'm so happy you scored that goal.' I began to feel better just talking about the game.

While I was swept up in the moment, I decided that it was time to come clean. I was sick of all these lies. I was just about to tell my parents about my football life when the club president entered from an adjoining room.

'Lucia, I'm so glad to see that you are safe. We were so worried about you.'

'Thanks. No need to worry, I'm back in one piece and ready to go home.' I was kind of relieved he'd stepped in. Maybe it wasn't the right moment to reveal all.

The president addressed Papa. 'Paolo, the media are sniffing around for interviews with Lucia about the incident. I've sorted them out. I've also organised for bodyguards to escort you to my helicopter, which will take you home. I told the police the doctor would have to examine Lucia at your home and he can talk to her when she's feeling up to it.'

'No, I want to get it over with now and put it all behind me! I want to go back to Australia. I don't want to stay here any more!' I surprised them all with my outburst and I even surprised myself.

Papa's response was reassuring. 'Lucia, you need to rest now. Let's go home and think about it. Don't worry, we're going to Sydney soon . . . we'll work it out.'

'Paolo, why don't you take some extra time off? Enjoy an extended holiday with the family in Australia and come back to prepare for the Champions League. The manager and players will support you on this. It's more important for you to be there for Frida and Lucia. I'll organise security for you and the family, here and for your stay in Australia.'

Papa didn't hesitate, 'Yes, you're right. My family is more important to me than anything else – this time football will just have to wait. Princess, your wish is my command.'

# Chapter 23

# Pesky paparazzi

The whole nation wanted to know my story. It was unbearable. To escape the invasion of the paparazzi, we headed straight for Lake Como. Papa's goal took a back seat while the media played with sensational headlines.

'Zoffi's daughter escapes death.' 'Lucia Zoffi held hostage.'

'The highs and lows of Paolo Zoffi.'

There was a huge media contingent parked outside our villa when we arrived, while helicopters hovered loudly above. The constant chopper noise added to our frustration at being kept prisoners in our own home.

My picture was plastered over every news and sports bulletin, as they competed for the most current story about the abduction. They used old footage of us out shopping, eating breakfast at our local restaurant, and walking along the street. They even had a shot of me at my local gelato shop with Gigi. And the weirdest thing: we were also told by friends that someone had managed to film me being chased by that awful woman while she fired her gun. It was on the internet. Why hadn't that person helped me? The police were investigating the footage. I hadn't seen it and I didn't want to.

The situation was making my parents more and more stressed. They decided that we'd fly out to Sydney as soon as possible. We were inundated with phone calls on Papa's private line from all of our friends, and even Italy's prime minister called Papa, asking after me. Things weren't helped by all the false reports in the media, like 'Zoffi turns his back on Italy'. It was all lies, typical media sensationalism.

All I wanted to do was put this scary incident behind me. One thing I'd learnt was that life was fleeting and it was time to pursue my dream for real. I couldn't wait to get back to Sydney and my friends there, even though it meant leaving Pino and my other Milano friends.

Before we could leave, I had to speak with the police. The abductors were still being held under police guard in hospital. I just wanted to get the police interviews out of the way so we could leave for Sydney without any further hitches. Thankfully, instead of us having to travel to the station, they came to our home.

Talking about the abduction was strange. I felt as though I was telling the police about another girl. I discussed every detail without emotion, although I didn't want my parents to hear everything. When I mentioned the abductor's attempted kiss, Mama couldn't take it and made an excuse to leave the room. Papa insisted on staying with me. He wouldn't leave my side, holding my hand as I spoke.

I was relieved when it was all over. Mama returned and came straight over to me with a huge hug. She was still quite emotional. 'Thank goodness we have you back home with us. I'm so proud of the way you've handled yourself. I have to ask . . .' she added. 'I meant to tell you earlier that your friend Bella called from Australia during your papa's game. She thought something was wrong when she tried to reach you and a stranger answered your mobile. Was that . . . was that one of the people who kidnapped you?' I nodded and her eyes filled with tears. 'Oh dear . . . I should have acted earlier, but I thought you were watching the game with your friend. I just thought Bella was overreacting. I'm so, so sorry,' she wept.

I hugged her again. 'No, Mama I'm sorry that I lied
to you. It's not your fault. But you did help me, with that hot-pink lippy.'

Mama forced a smile. 'Clever girl. See, everything has its place. I'm glad it came in handy.'

'Yes, you helped save me, Mama. And you were right, all girls should be armed with lipstick.'

We laughed.

# Chapter 24

# Fantasy game

'Ciao Bella, it's Lucy.'

'Are you all right? I've been so worried about you. Everyone's worried about you, especially your grandparents and the boys. What happened at your dad's game?'

'It's a long story. It's been a nightmare and I'm too exhausted to talk about it right now. I'll fill you in when I get back to Sydney. I can't wait to get away from here. It's out of control . . . the media won't leave us alone.'

'The news about the abduction is all over the TV and newspapers here in Sydney.'

'Oh no! Being in the news in Australia is the last thing I want! I was hoping to escape all of that. Please say hi to the boys for me and tell them that I'm fine and eager to come back and play. One more thing – what's happened to Max? Do you have any news?'

'That's why I called you before. Max has been found but he's in a lot of trouble.'

'What's wrong with him? Where is he?'

'You won't believe it. He was in emergency and right now he's in police custody. He was found by the side of the road at Rushcutters Bay, unconscious and with a broken nose.'

'Oh, poor Max. What's going to happen to him now?' 'We're not sure . . . it's hard to get any information because we're not related.'

'Can't you use your mother's influence? We've got to make sure that he's looked after.'

'Yes, don't worry, I'm a step ahead . . . Mum organised a very good lawyer to represent Max and she said that we'll be able to visit him soon. The police are investigating him running away from his foster home, but they're also talking to him about that guy he hit. Mum has offered to be his guardian in the interim, and the lawyer is trying to push that through quickly. Then Max can stay with us for a little while instead of being sent to a juvenile detention centre or back to foster care or whatever.'

'It all sounds so messy, but thank heavens for your mama. I'll be getting into Sydney late tomorrow night, so I'll try to visit the following day.'

'Can't wait to see you. We're so relieved you're okay.

Call me as soon as you arrive. See ya!' 'I can't wait to see you too. Ciao!'

We were given a police escort to the airport but of course that didn't stop the paparazzi from following us in cars and motorbikes. We were travelling at high speeds and even ran some red lights, but the photographers were just relentless.

I was relieved when we made it to the airport, although it was swarming with police. It was spooky, and I couldn't wait to board the jet.

'Papa, this is scary. Can we please hurry? And do we have to have these men in black suits surrounding us?'

'Yes, my beautiful girl. All this extra security is for our benefit. It's nothing for you to worry about. I just want you to relax and enjoy the flight,' he said softly.

We were driven onto the tarmac to the waiting jet, while the media scrum was blocked from travelling any further. I was relieved to be beyond their reach and on our way to Sydney.

'*Buongiorno*, Signor Zoffi, Signora and Signorina Zoffi and little Gigi. Welcome aboard,' the captain greeted us. 'We have good weather forecast, so you should enjoy a relaxing flight.'

I put Gigi in her special dog box at the back of the plane. Luckily Mama's assistant had managed to pull a few strings, so Gigi didn't have to spend months locked up in quarantine. That would have been horrible.

I couldn't wait to lie down and shut myself off from the rest of the world. I knew I had to try and leave that frightening ordeal behind me, but it was hard to wipe it from my mind. The sooner I got to Sydney and played some football, the better. That would help shut out those awful memories. I also had to make sure that Papa fell in love with Sydney, because I was starting to think I'd want to stay there forever. I wanted to be with my grandparents and leave Italy behind me; as much as I loved it, I didn't think I could face going back.

I closed my eyes and focused on my fantasy football game. I saw myself back playing alongside Zinedine Zidane. My team had just been awarded a penalty after I was taken down inside the box. Just like before, Zizou wanted me to take the penalty. I took my lucky five steps back and was about to take a crack at the ball, when suddenly I felt like I was being shaken.

'Lucia, it's time to wake up, we're about to land. You must buckle up, sleeping beauty,' Mama demanded.

Oh no, not again. I didn't want to leave this game. But the image was gone, so I reluctantly opened my eyes.

'I thought I'd only nodded off for a few minutes. Did I sleep the whole way?' I asked wearily.

'Yes, you were in a deep sleep. You missed all the meals but we didn't want to disturb you. Even Gigi's barking didn't wake you. We thought you could do with the rest,' replied Papa.

Gigi really was making some noise. 'She's hard to ignore now,' I said, as I tickled her through the wire of her dog box. 'And please don't forget, Mama, Papa: it's Lucy now that we're in Australia. Please call me Lucy, just like my friends,' I said with a grin and clicked on my seatbelt.

# Chapter 25

# La dolce vita

We arrived on a warm and still Sydney night, welcomed by a vast sparkling blanket of shining stars . . . a magnificent greeting from the harbour city.

'Signor Zoffi, Signora and Signorina Zoffi, welcome to Sydney. Your driver is standing by to take you to your hotel. I've been alerted that there's a media contingent waiting out the front, so you'll be taken along the back route. Nonetheless, please be on your guard. Take it easy and good luck. Ciao,' said the captain.

'Why are we staying in a hotel? I want to see Grandpa and Nanna,' I demanded, still a little drowsy from my long nap.

'Lucy, it's too late to go to their place now,' Papa replied. 'We'll see them tomorrow morning. We don't want the media snooping around their home, so it's probably best to keep away for now.'

'You're right. I just miss them. I know one thing for sure – I'm starving. Let's get something to eat.' I noticed Mama staring into space. 'Mama, are you okay?'

'I can't wait to see your Nanna and Grandpa either, but things may be different this time. We won't be staying with them, since they don't have that much room. And as Papa said, we don't want the media prying into their lives. Right now, I just want you to take it easy. You've been through enough. Let's go to the hotel and have a lovely meal.' Mama was still looking out into the distance.

She obviously had a lot more on her mind than she was admitting, but it was too late to delve any further. They were right; I didn't want Nanna and Grandpa caught up in this craziness.

It was a strange ride to the hotel as we sped along the back streets, trying to keep away from the media. How did they know we were here?

As soon as we arrived at the hotel, waiting photographers swarmed into our path. Click, click, click. It was so intense that we couldn't get out of the car until the hotel staff ordered them away.

We were taken to the top floor and given adjoining rooms. It was bliss being tucked away in the room, especially when our hearty meals arrived. We barely spoke as we devoured our food. After a long bath, I could feel my energy waning. I was exhausted.

I jumped into my king-size bed while my parents retired into the next room. I was so tired, yet I still found it hard to fall asleep. I had to leave the light on, because the abduction kept playing out in my mind. I still had so many questions.

Why did they do it? How could people become so desperate? Why did he apologise to me before he was shot?

Then my mind wandered to poor Max . . . I had to see him.

Next morning I awoke with a heavy weight on my shoulders. I still felt totally drained, but at least I was going to be reunited with Nanna and Grandpa. I couldn't wait.

Sydney put on its best face – the sun was smiling down on us as Mama asked the driver to take us on a little scenic tour on the way to the Cross.

We headed for the underbelly of the Harbour Bridge, in the oldest part of town known as The Rocks. The water glistened with a layer of silver sprinkles while boats and yachts glided along its silky surface. The famous sails of the Opera House dominated the harbour's skyline. As far as Papa was concerned, Sydney had scored the opening goal.

'Spectacular! This city is like a gorgeous woman resting in the warm sun. It's remarkable, despite the rats with the cameras. I'm looking forward to seeing more of it, especially its famous beaches.' Papa was obviously smitten with this new woman.

We drove by the Woolloomooloo wharf. The luxurious cruisers moored against a gallery of upmarket restaurants also sparked Papa's interest. 'Now, I like this set-up. It reminds me of Cannes or parts of

Monaco, but on a more intimate scale,' he said, and then he yelled, '*La dolce vita!* – the sweet life.'

We wound up the hill and towards the tree-lined streets at the back of the Cross, past beautiful old terrace houses and trendy restaurants. We made a special detour to one of our favourite haunts.

Mama jumped in before me. 'Paolo, Lucy and I mostly dine here at Paradiso. It's owned by an Italian family who are very hospitable and accommodating. I know you'll love it here.'

'Yes, Papa, maybe we can eat here tonight. One of the owners, Enrico, is a huge AC Milan fan. He knows I have a soft spot for dark chocolate, so he always brings me an extra serving. And they have the most delicious calamari – it's even better than back home.' I was hoping to make the trip to my grandparents' even more appealing.

Papa was convinced. 'Okay you two, you know how to win me over. I can tell I'm going to like it here.'

# Chapter 26

# Men in black

'Nanna, Grandpa,' I shouted as I ran into their arms. They joined me in a tearful reunion while Gigi licked everyone excitedly.

'We were so worried about you. Thank goodness you're safe,' Nanna said, tightening her squeeze while tears poured down her cheeks.

'I was so worried about *you*! But you look good,' I mumbled, trying to control my tears.

'Lucy, my princess,' Grandpa cried. 'We're fine, and your Nanna's getting back to her best. We were so frightened when we heard about the kidnapping. You're not going back to that place, it's much safer here with us.'

'Well, we'll talk about all of that later,' said Papa. 'Tony, Betty, it's good to see you both looking so healthy.'

'We're better now that Lucy's back. And we're so happy to see you and Frida here, Paolo. I just don't know what we would have done if Lucy . . .' Grandpa held me so tight I was nearly struggling for air.

'Why don't we close the shop for a few hours so that we can go up the road for brunch and just relax. I think we could all do with a break,' Mama suggested.

'I have lots of food upstairs waiting to be devoured, including my famous tiramisu. And I have some fresh coffee brewing, so let's relax here,' said Nanna.

'Yum, thanks Nanna. I can't wait to dig in,' I jumped in, eager to get upstairs and plough into her delectable cooking.

Mama joined in the hug, 'Thanks Mum, it's just what we need. I think your home-cooked food will do the trick. It's good to be back home.'

Looking over Mama's shoulder, I noticed a black car with heavily tinted windows parked directly across the road. Two men dressed in black suits and wrap-around sunnies were leaning against the car. They reminded me of the guys in that alien movie, *Men in Black* . . . freaky! But these guys didn't look as cool as Hollywood actors. In fact, they looked very suspicious; I was sure they were watching us. Or was I just being paranoid?

'Papa have you noticed that black car parked across the road with the strange-looking guys staring at us?' I asked.

'Yes, I was hoping you wouldn't notice them. They're our bodyguards. They'll follow us, day and night. It's a security measure, just for now, but I don't want you worrying about it. They're here to protect us, but if they are bothering you, I'll tell them to keep their distance,' said Papa.

Great, that was all I needed . . . security following my every move. How would I play football with these guys on my tail?

'But Papa, we're safe here. It's spooky to think that we're being watched 24/7. It's bad enough being hounded by the paparazzi, without being followed by bodyguards as well. Can't you tell them to go away? Please!'

'Right, let's go upstairs. I can't wait to get into Nanna's tucker. Come on, Lucy, I'll race you,' said Grandpa with a frown, eager to change the subject.

We bolted up the stairs, and I lay on the cosy lounge and cuddled into my favourite cushion, one that Nanna had made me, with my name embroidered across a big red heart. I looked around the comfortable little apartment, enjoying the safety and warmth of being back here with my family. It was even more special now with Papa and my pup here.

After tucking into a feast, we got stuck into Nanna's specialty. I always left room for her tiramisu . . . it's too delicious!

'My goodness Lucy, I don't know where you put it. It's a good thing you go to plenty of dance classes. It's great to see you enjoy my cooking, bless you,' said Nanna.

'Didn't you know that Italians live for food? I'm just staying true to my culture.' We laughed as I patted my stomach.

We were all enjoying dessert and being together again as a family, but I was still determined to get an answer from Papa about the freaks outside. I had to get rid of the security guards pronto. They could make my life hell.

I walked up to the window and peeped out from behind the long floral curtains. 'Papa, look, they're still outside. Are you going to tell them to go away?'

'Lucy, I told you not to worry about them. They're just doing their job. I'll tell them to be a little less conspicuous, just to keep you happy,' he replied.

I'd just have to accept the situation, for now at least. I couldn't raise any suspicion about my motive for getting rid of them. I'd have to be smarter with my movements. I reached over for another serving of tiramisu.

'Okay, Papa. I won't mention it again. I suppose it's better to be safe than sorry,' I said, trying to sound grateful.

'Oh Lucy, I nearly forgot to tell you,' Grandpa said as he was digging into his second helping. 'Harry dropped in asking after you. When you feel up to it you should give him a call. He was worried about you and he has a lot of news to share.'

'Thanks Grandpa. I'll give him a call,' I cautiously replied.

'Who's Harry?' Papa asked, looking strained.

'He's just one of my friends,' I said quietly. I knew what Papa thought about me being friends with boys, so I tried to downplay it.

'I told you to watch out for boys, especially the ones that claim they're your friends,' insisted my overprotective papa.

'Relax, Paolo. Harry's a good kid. I've known him since he was a baby. You can trust him,' said Grandpa.

Papa nodded and looked at me. 'I don't trust any boy, but if Grandpa thinks he's harmless, then I guess it's okay for you to see him, as long as I can meet him.'

'Papa, you can meet Harry soon – and *thanks* for giving me permission to see one of my best friends.' Oh my goodness! That reminded me – I hadn't called Pino yet! 'May I be excused? I'd like to make a few calls.'

'Why don't you call your friends later? You need to rest after the long flight.'

'Paolo, let her be. Chatting with her friends will probably help Lucy get her mind off other things,' suggested Grandpa.

Mama, surprisingly, backed him up. 'Yes, Paolo, I agree, it's a good idea.'

Papa was persuaded. 'Okay, I've been outvoted.' I hugged him. 'Thanks Papa, you're the best.'

I gave him a kiss on the cheek, and kissed the rest of the family, and then I grabbed my bag and went into my grandparents' bedroom to make my phone calls. It was only when I reached for the phone that I remembered it was the middle of the night in Italy, and Bella would be at school. I'd have to make my calls later. For the meantime, I had a lot to think about. How could I tell Papa about the Lions? I sat down on the bed and made myself comfortable.

As much as I stewed over my dilemma, I simply couldn't think of a way to tell Papa and Mama about the Lions and the Champion of Champions that wouldn't freak them out. This was ridiculous. I had my family all together at last – I should go and actually spend some time with them. I raced into the lounge room. It was empty.

I wandered downstairs and heard Mama's voice coming from the shop. 'We'd actually already bought a house before all this happened. It's on the other side of the bay in Darling Point, so we'll be nice and close. I want to set up a home for Lucy to help her adjust during our stay, since we're not sure how long we'll be here. Of course, it's all happened so quickly we've barely had time to think, but we need to consider our future. We'd always thought it would be in Italy, but it's all changed since Lucy was abducted, and since your accident, Mum. Oh, it's great to see how you've bounced back so quickly. It must be Grandpa's cooking.' They all laughed gently at that.

Then Papa spoke. 'My career has always been in Italy, but I'm preparing to retire from the national team soon, so I can spend more time with my girls. It's been on the cards for a while. I also know that Lucy wants more time with all of us, especially her grandparents, and that's swaying our decision to spend more time here.'

Oh, this was amazing. Sometimes I loved Mama's spontaneity. A house in Sydney would be ideal. I could see Nanna and Grandpa every day, and Papa cutting back his football commitments would give us more family time.

I kept my ear glued to the door but was set off-balance as it swung open. I quickly regained my composure, hoping I looked as though I'd just been about to walk in. 'Lucy, I hope you weren't eavesdropping.' Grandpa sounded stern but had a big grin.

'Oh no, of course not, I was just looking for you,' I said, a little sheepishly.

'Well, we're going to take a long walk to get Paolo acquainted with the city and then we'll have dinner at Paradiso. Run up and have a quick wash, princess, then we'll go,' he said.

'Bella, it's me, Lucy.'

'I couldn't wait to talk to you. Are you okay?'

'I'm jet-lagged, but okay really. We've had a really relaxed day. All I've done is walk around and eat . . . I'm stuffed! Anyway, how are you? And what's the latest on Max?'

'Oh, I'm fine. Max was released by the police after being questioned. They've allowed him to come home with us while they continue investigating his case. We've got interim guardianship and that means he doesn't have to go into some sort of foster home – for now, anyway. I think he's dying with embarrassment now that everyone knows he's a street kid. Dylan and Harry feel bad but they're a bit confused, I think . . . they're still angry about the fight and his walk-out on the team.'

Bella paused for a moment. 'Everyone was so concerned about you, Lucy, even Max. But his attitude isn't helping things. He's being a real pain.'

'He'll get over it. It's wild that your mum has basically become Max's angel.'

'Mum may be busy, but when a kid needs help, especially someone that we know, she does her best. Max was in Dylan's team for years and they used to hang out together, so she's known him for ages. She's really upset that she had no idea about his life on the streets. He's always been really secretive. Even Dylan barely knew anything about him. He's certainly changed since I last saw him – he's very cute now, even if he is a pain sometimes.'

Oh, I hoped Bella didn't like him . . . but why should I care?

'Well he's okay, but he is a bit of a wild one. Your mum's amazing. Would it be okay if I came over tomorrow to catch up with you and the boys?'

'Of course, I'm dying to see you and I want to find out more about what happened in Italy. The papers have made up all sorts of crazy stories. One said that a terrorist organisation was behind your abduction and that guns were fired. Anyway, let's talk about it when I see you. It sounds like a really frightening experience.'

'Yeah, I felt as though I was starring in a scary horror film. It was terrifying. I appreciate what I have much more now. All I want to do is see you and the boys and play football.'

'Ha! Well, I can't wait to see you either. Come around after breakfast.'

'Perfect! Ciao, Bella. Good night.' 'Night, Lucy. Ciao.'

I put the phone down and groaned at my full belly. It had been a good day. Papa had loved walking around the city and seemed to have found a new friend in Enrico. At the restaurant they'd talked about football and compared the lifestyles of Milan and Sydney. Papa was starting to settle in very nicely.

# Chapter 27

# The Zoffi secret

'So, you're off to see Bella. I'm looking forward to meeting her and her family,' said Papa, as I got ready to leave the next morning.

'You'll get to meet them soon, Papa, but right now I'm in a hurry. I've kept Bella waiting long enough!' I explained anxiously.

I was also a little nervous about seeing the boys. Now they'd know all about my family, thanks to the media. I wouldn't be just Lucy Zeezou the footballer, I'd be back to 'Lucia Zoffi, daughter of football legend Paolo Zoffi.'

'Lucy, wait, are you sure you'll be all right on your own?' Mama asked. 'Maybe we should come with you.'

'Oh really, Mama, I'm fine. It's a beautiful day – why don't you show Papa around the beaches? He kept saying yesterday that he's desperate to see them. Isn't that right, Papa?'

Mama answered before he could. 'All right then, but just remember you're not to venture elsewhere. Come straight home from Bella's, and call us when you're on your way. The driver will wait for you until you're ready to leave.'

'Don't worry! I promise I'll call you. Ciao!'

It was a relief to finally get into the car and have some time to myself. All I could think about now was seeing my friends, especially Max. My stomach was fluttering with the anticipation of our reunion. Weird.

I was so caught up in my thoughts that I hadn't noticed what was going on outside the car. 'Please put your seatbelt on, Signorina Zoffi,' the driver said. 'A paparazzo is following us. He's already taken shots of you getting into the car.' The driver put his weight on the accelerator as he negotiated the streets at speed.

Didn't he have anything better to do than follow a fourteen-year-old girl? I could understand them wanting happy snaps of Papa – but *me*? It was ridiculous! I called Bella on the mobile and alerted her to the paparazzo in pursuit.

'Bella, it's me, Lucy. I'm on my way to your place but we're being followed by a photographer. He's probably here for the Italian press. It's madness.'

'I'll make sure the security gate is on standby for your approach. Don't worry, we've dealt with this kind of thing before. You'll be fine.'

'Okay, thanks. Ciao.'

Moments after the driver finally managed to lose the photographer, we were within sight of Bella's house. As we approached the driveway the huge gates parted and we drove straight in. I was relieved to be safe behind them and away from prying eyes.

The house's large double doors swung open and an excited Bella appeared with a huge grin. She squealed, 'It's so good to see you. Thank heavens you're here safe and sound.' She pulled back a little and smiled at me. 'I took the liberty of inviting the jock, Harry, over. The things you do for your friends! Of course, Max and Dylan are also here and so's my mum. She can't wait to meet you.'

'Wow, your mum's here, I thought she'd be at work,' I said, surprised.

'Well, she wants to make sure that you and your family are settling in without any problems. She'll probably talk to your parents too, to see if they need any help, just because she can pull a few strings if need be.'

It was good of Bella's mum to be so concerned, but I just wanted to hang out with the guys. I was over talking about the whole dire experience. I just wanted to forget about it . . . although the boys would probably also want to hear my side of the story.

'Mum's waiting to see you now because she only has half an hour before she has to rush off to a meeting and then a press conference.' Bella rolled her eyes.

We walked into the depths of the house and on into a library lined with books. The shelves climbed the walls right up to the ceiling, and an antique wooden ladder was perched in the corner. I took a closer look . . . politics and history dominated the spines of many of the titles at eye level. In an adjoining room, an attractive petite woman in a tailored yet feminine cream suit sat at a long antique desk, typing on a laptop.

Bella's face lit up when she saw her mum. She headed straight over to her, kissed her on the cheek, and announced, 'Mum, this is my best friend Lucy Zoffi . . . Lucy, this is my mum, Helen.'

'It's an honour to meet you, Mrs Jones,' I said.

I met high-profile people all the time but my best friend's mama – a leader of a major political party and the state premier . . . that was pretty cool. She had the power to make decisions affecting people's lives. I couldn't understand why Bella dreamt of being in front of the camera when she had such an inspiring role model.

They had a strong resemblance, with their shoulder-length straight black hair and beautiful flawless skin, thanks to their Chinese heritage – the surname came from Helen's Welsh ex-husband. Mrs Jones' soft brown eyes peered out of reading glasses sitting on the edge of her small nose. She was just missing the braces, otherwise they could have been sisters.

She addressed me with a deep, calm voice. 'Please call me Helen. I'm very pleased to meet you, Lucy. I've heard so much about you. Bella doesn't usually hang out with sporty types, but I gather there's more to you than meets the eye. Now tell me, is your family planning to stay in Sydney for long?'

'I think so. It depends on Papa's football, but I think they're leaning that way. I think we'll at least be coming here more regularly, because of what happened to me, and my grandparents' health. They're still working it out. 'I love it here because I've made such good friends, especially Bella. And it's much more relaxed here . . . well, it was. Right now I feel safer in your country.'

'That's good to hear. I can't imagine how frightened you must have been when you were abducted. Are you up to telling us about it?' she gently enquired.

'Um, yes, but it's still being investigated. All I know is that I was abducted for ransom money. There are all sorts of stories being thrown around, but the police in Italy are handling everything. I do know that the kidnappers were desperate and not awfully bright.'

I recounted the events. They were still very fresh in my mind, although it was hard to believe that it had all happened only a few days ago. Bella and her mama gasped and nodded with concern until we were interrupted.

'Please excuse me. Helen, your car is ready to take you to your next meeting. And your brief has been prepared for the press conference.'

Helen approached me and said, 'Lucy, thank you for sharing your story, and it was a pleasure to meet you. I hope you'll be a regular guest in our home. We'll have your family over for dinner one night after everything settles down. Hope to see you soon.' She hugged Bella and me, then strolled out of the room.

'Thank you. Bye!' was all I could muster.

Butterflies madly fluttered in my stomach, as if they were desperate to escape and be free. It was time to see the boys . . . Bella must have sensed my trepidation, as she grabbed me by the arm and led me upstairs to the living area.

'Come on, the boys are looking forward to seeing you, especially Dylan. I think he still has a crush on you. He made sure he was free to see you today.' She teasingly nudged me as we climbed the winding staircase.

I was fighting a rush of blood to my face. What was I going to say? I wished I could just face them on the football pitch, then I'd know what to say and do. Put me on the pitch and I moved like a dolphin, effortlessly gliding in its habitat. Out here, I was a fish out of water, struggling for breath.

I walked in with Bella and saw them challenging each other at an electronic football game, buying and selling players for their teams.

'Um, guys, look who's here!' Bella said, trying to grab their attention.

They looked up and stared at me as if I had two heads. There was an uncomfortable silence until finally Dylan attempted to break the ice.

'Wow, I mean hey, Lucy, how are you?' He looked at me nervously, although that was more welcoming than either Harry or Max.

'I'm fine. Congratulations for reaching the final of the Champion of Champions. How's the preparation going?' I tried not to look embarrassed as Dylan continued to stare. I hoped that prompting football talk would warm the room.

Harry and Max still hadn't said anything, and Dylan was left to reply. 'We've been training really hard. We have another session tomorrow before Sunday's kick-off. Do you think you're ready to train after what's happened?'

'Of course, I can't wait to get onto the pitch.'

'You must have had a kick around in Italy with your famous dad, *Paolo Zoffi*.' Harry didn't look up from the game, but I could see his scowl clearly enough.

'Yeah, Lucy . . . you're so lucky that your dad is an international football legend. No wonder you're such a good player.' Dylan added with enthusiasm.

This is what I was afraid of from the beginning: 'Lucy's cool because of her papa.' My identity was out the window. And, to make it worse, Max hadn't said a thing. He hadn't even made eye contact. Maybe he was just in pain, I told myself, looking at all the bandages around his left arm and nose.

'It's no big deal really. He doesn't have time to kick the ball with me. He's either training most of the time or he's busy with his business. In fact, I'm lucky if I see him at breakfast,' I replied cautiously, hoping they'd leave it at that.

Max awoke from his silence. *'Not a big deal.* How can you say that? Your dad just happens to be one of the best footballers on the planet. Yet another Lucy secret. Why can't you just tell the truth? You know we all love our football, that's all we talk about. As if we wouldn't want to know about Paolo Zoffi. He's living our dream.'

I was stunned, but I wasn't in the mood for an argument. I'd hoped that the boys would be a little more welcoming. So here I was, back to being Paolo Zoffi's daughter. Just like in Italy, Lucy had to take a back seat. I was shattered.

Bella must have taken a look at my face just then. 'Hey, guys, I think you're being harsh. Lucy's recovering from a horrible experience, she's lucky to be alive and all you can talk about is her dad and why she didn't tell you about him! I don't blame her for not sharing it. Don't you think you should ask about how she's feeling after being abducted for ransom by lunatics with guns? Or how she escaped by breaking a door down with her snappy football kick? Or how she's coping with the prying paparazzi?'

That caught their attention.

Bella's rant continued. 'I thought we were her friends, her best friends. And Max, after Lucy was rescued, all she was concerned about was your safety – and this is how you welcome her back!'

Dylan threw Max a snarly look. 'She's not the only one with secrets, Max.'

Max became fidgety and unsettled.

Bella wasn't finished yet. 'Oh, this is a waste of time. You're all just a bunch of insensitive jocks. You should be ashamed of yourselves!'

The room fell silent. The boys looked embarrassed and stared at the floor.

But I was the one who should really feel ashamed . . .

I'd lied to my friends from the beginning.

Bella grabbed my hand and led me to the door.

Finally Dylan said, 'Wait, Lucy. Please wait. We're sorry. Bella's right, we should have been more thoughtful. I suppose we just got carried away. Of course we were worried about you, and we're glad that you're back.'

'No Dylan, I'm the one who ought to be sorry. I should have told you about him from the beginning, but in Italy my identity is overshadowed by Papa's celebrity. I just wanted my own life and to be liked for being me, not for being the daughter of a famous person. I was enjoying being anonymous for the first time in my life, but I know I should have told you. I'm sorry for hurting your feelings.' My eyes welled up. I tried to hold the tears back but I had no control, and they rolled down my face.

I ran out, looking for a place to hide.

# Chapter 28

# Celebrity obsession

I sat on Bella's bed in tears, confused and angry about what had just happened. Couldn't I just be accepted for who I was? Why was it so important for people to be around someone famous? We were just like everybody else, really. Even if we had more material possessions, we still did the same things, wanted the same things. Why couldn't people see that? The one thing I wanted to pursue more than anything was out of my reach. Like a bird with clipped wings.

'Lucy, what you said back there was beautiful. It'll be okay, I promise. They missed you and were very concerned about you. To the boys you'll always be Zeezou, no matter who your father is . . . they just don't know how to tell you. Remember, they're jocks and boys. They have no idea.' Bella rolled her eyes again.

She continued, 'They're shocked that they're so close to football royalty, you must understand that. Harry and Max were in contact with Dylan and me all the time after they found out that you'd been abducted. Anyway, this should be a time to be happy. You're free and safe now and ready to kick butt in the soccer final.'

I laughed at that. 'Bella, you're such a good friend. That speech you made to the boys was amazing. Thank you! One thing that's bothering me though – you've got to call it football, not soccer! But yes, I can't wait to kick butt . . . and not *just* on the pitch!'

'That's the spirit. Let's go back and see the boys. We'll start again,' Bella urged.

I didn't want to leave just yet. I didn't want to face any more questions, either. Before I could say another word, there was a knock on the door.

'Bella, Lucy, can we please come in?' yelled Harry.

I decided I was going to let them stew for a bit. 'No, we're busy. Go away.'

Harry took the lead again, 'Please, Lucy, Bella, let us in. We have a big problem.'

Bella and I looked at each other anxiously. 'Okay then, come in.'

Harry and Dylan entered Bella's very girlie pink bed-room, distracted by the walls covered with pictures of glamorous models and famous actors. They looked a bit stunned – surely Bella's bedroom couldn't be that bad?

Dylan finally spoke. 'Max has taken off. We were in the kitchen getting a snack while he waited on the balcony. When we came back he was gone. We've searched the whole estate, the grounds, everywhere we could think of, but there's no sign of him. Mum's going to be furious.'

Bella calmly took control. 'We all need to think hard about what we're going to do. If we raise the alarm, Max will probably be caught and taken to the police and arrested for trying to run away while his case is still being investigated. Also, Mum's position could be compromised if word gets out about this. The media will have a field day. We must keep this a secret and we must find him.'

We were interrupted by my phone ringing. I sighed when I saw the number, but answered anyway.

'Lucy, are you done at Bella's? Papa and I have some news for you.'

'What is it, Mama?' I was intrigued. What now?

'Oh, it's too big to say over the phone. Get home soon, okay?'

*More* news? I'd had enough excitement for a lifetime. But Mama sounded happy, so I didn't want to ruin her mood. I started saying goodbye to Bella and the boys.

'Lucy, before you go – we're really sorry for being so harsh. All this news has been a big shock but we're happy you're back. We'll find Max, don't worry,' Harry reassured me, while Dylan nodded in agreement.

It was just what I needed to hear. Bella gave Harry an encouraging look, as if to say wow, you're not a total jock after all.

I was so relieved I was part of the team again.

I walked out to the car with Bella. 'Bye, Bella. I hope to hear from you soon,' I said, trying not to say anything that would let the driver guess I was talking about Max. 'I'll call you as soon as I have news,' she said coolly.

'Anyway, I'll try to drop over to your training session tomorrow with Dylan.'

'Great, see you soon. Ciao!'

I was so worried about Max. I peered out the window as we headed away from Bella's home, hoping to spot him. Surely he couldn't be far from here.

But there was no sign of him. As we drove away from the house I decided to make a quick detour.

'Could you please pull over into that park that overlooks the harbour? I'd like to enjoy the view for a moment. Thank you.'

I hoped he was hiding around here. It was a long shot, but I didn't know what else I could do. I had a quick walk around, trying to look as though I was enjoying the scenery. But there was no one in sight.

I walked back towards the car. Suddenly I noticed a banging noise. The driver was in the car singing along to the radio, oblivious. I moved closer to the car and the sound grew stronger. It seemed to be coming from the boot.

I interrupted the driver. 'Excuse me, could you please open the boot? I need to get something out.' He nodded and pressed a button.

It popped open. I looked in and had to stop myself from screaming.

# Chapter 29

# Heartbeat

My heart was pounding so fast that I thought it was going to leap out. I was excited and relieved all at once. At least Max was safe and unharmed – but what should I do now? I didn't know what it was about Max, but he made me feel funny . . . kind of nervous and happy at the same time. He could have been more welcoming at Bella's, but I loved the way he could seem so sure of himself and fearless in other ways. He was a risk-taker. And it didn't hurt that he was cute and a very talented footballer. 'Lucy!' he whispered, putting his finger over my lips.

'Don't say a word, gently close the boot so that I can hold it down . . . it'll make it easier for me to get out when we arrive at your place, and it would be good to get a little air. Quick, get back in the car so you don't raise any suspicion.'

I gave him the thumbs up and followed his instructions.

'Everything all right, Ms Zoffi?' asked the driver. 'Oh, yes, fine thanks. I just want to get home now,'

I said in my best calm voice.

I didn't know whether to text Bella or wait for further instructions from Max. He probably had a plan. I'd just wait until we got to my grandparents' shop and decide then. My heart was racing and my legs a little shaky, but it was such a relief to know that he was safe and with me.

I couldn't wait to get home and see his face again. What had come over me? I'd never felt this eager to see anyone.

The driver interrupted my thoughts, and I realised the car had stopped. 'Excuse me, Ms Zoffi, we're home.'

Max . . . I had to get him out of the boot before anyone saw him.

'Thank you. I'll just get my bag out,' I replied. I jumped out and headed to the back of the car.

'I'll get it, Ms Zoffi,' the driver said as he opened his door.

'No, it's okay. I'll take care of it. Thank you anyway,' I insisted, but when I lifted the boot to help Max out, my heart skipped a beat. He was gone . . . yet another disappearing act. I frantically looked around.

'Is everything all right, Ms Zoffi?' the driver asked suspiciously. I looked up and saw him watching me. I really had to settle my nerves.

'Oh yes, all fine. Thank you. See you tomorrow.' I tried to look calm as I closed the boot.

I was worried about Max, but also angry that he had left without telling me what he was doing and where he was going. He could at least have waited for me. How was I supposed to know he was okay? For all I knew, the bodyguards could have seen him escape. Maybe they'd captured him, even. I just had to hope that he'd managed to slip away unseen.

I moved towards the front door of Grandpa's shop, trying to look casual, while my eyes anxiously circled the area for any sign of Max.

Before I could go inside I was startled by a whisper. 'Don't look this way, Zeezou. Meet me at the Reg once it's dark.'

# Chapter 30

# Houdini

Grandpa welcomed me with open arms as I entered the shop. I was wrapped up in safe arms, something Max didn't get to experience. I decided to tell Grandpa about Max's disappearing act. I knew he'd been concerned about him too.

'Grandpa, I need your help,' I nervously requested. He gave me a reassuring look, 'Of course, what is it,

princess?'

'It's Max. I know where he is but I'm not sure how to help him. I think the police may be after him, because he's escaped from Bella's place.'

I recounted the day's events, giving him every detail so that he fully understood the situation.

'Oh dear, that's not good. We have to handle this carefully. We need a good plan. Does anyone else know of his whereabouts?'

'I don't think so, unless those creepy bodyguards caught sight of him escaping from the boot. But I don't think they did. He's like that old illusionist, Houdini – one minute he's there, the next he's gone. I'm supposed to meet him at the Reg once it gets dark.' I wasn't quite sure how Grandpa would respond to this news, but I knew I couldn't keep it a secret.

Grandpa nodded. 'I think the best idea is to get him back to Bella's place as soon as possible. We need to talk him into going back – but don't you go running around the Reg at night on your own, Lucy. You know we're trying to keep you extra safe at the moment. I'll come with you tomorrow. If he wants to see you, I'm sure we'll find him. Now, why don't you run up and see your Mama and Papa. They're dying to tell you their news.'

I was relieved to have Grandpa's support, but I had to see Max tonight. I'd have to do the next part on my own. 'Thanks Grandpa. I don't know what I'd do without you.'

I headed upstairs, desperately trying to figure out how to escape tonight.

'Lucy, we're glad you're home. How was it catching up with your friends?' said Mama, while Nanna gave me a big hug.

Nanna didn't want to let me go. 'Nanna what's wrong?

Why are you crying?' I asked.

'Oh, I'm just so happy to have you here. I wish you could stay,' she mumbled.

'What do you mean, Nanna? I'm not going anywhere,' I assured her.

Mama stepped in. 'Well, Lucy, that's what I wanted to talk to you about. We're moving –'

I jumped in before she could finish her sentence. 'Moving where? I thought we were going to stay here, especially after what's happened.' I put on my best surprised expression.

'Well, it's all very exciting, Your nanna's just being a drama queen – actresses, they're all the same! We've bought a big beautiful house on the water just across the bay at Darling Point, only about a ten-minute walk from here. And we're thinking that we'll probably spend half our time here and the other half in Italy from now on. Of course, we'll be working it around Papa's football season and your school holidays. I know we'll manage somehow. We'll move into our new house in a few weeks' time, once everything's ready.'

'Oh, as long as we're close to Nanna and Grandpa then I'm happy.' I was too preoccupied with trying to work out tonight's escape to be very concerned about future plans. Judging by their expressions, my nonchalant response took them both by surprise. 'Where's Papa?' I asked, trying to change the subject.

'Papa's out with Enrico. They've been doing a tour of all the local Italian haunts, and now they're at his restaurant. Papa wants us to join him for dinner.'

I was so anxious about Max during dinner that I could hardly eat. Nanna noticed and gave me some worried looks. I whispered that I would explain everything later. I didn't think Grandpa had told her about Max yet.

As soon as we got home, I said I was tired and going to bed. Papa squeezed my shoulder.

'All right, darling girl. But tomorrow we'll spend a bit more time with you, yes?'

'Of course, Papa.'

I ran into the bedroom, closed the door behind me and bolted to the window to inspect a way out. I was afraid of heights but this was my only choice, so I swung out and grabbed a long thick pipe which weaved its way down the wall, finishing up a few metres from the ground. With my legs firmly wrapped around the pipe I scaled down it just like Spiderman (well, Spidergirl).

It was quite dark now, but the streetlights cast enough light for me to see what I was doing. I made it down undetected, although I was sure my heartbeat could be heard for miles.

I then had to jump the high back fence. I pretended I was leaping for the ball in the goal mouth, desperate to score, and on my second attempt I produced the winner. The jump had injected a rush of adrenalin, and with renewed vigour I dropped into the bushes below, scraping my legs in the process.

Unperturbed, I ran out onto the street. The sound of tennis balls being bashed over nets vibrated into the night behind me. I wasn't far from Max now . . . it wouldn't be long until we sorted out the next move. I crossed the road, bubbling with nerves.

There were quite a few people taking their dogs for a walk, but no sign of Max. Where was he? Now my heart was really racing as I headed to my favourite spot. The pitch was perfectly manicured and looked extremely inviting. I wished I had a ball: I'd be on the park in a flash.

As if on demand, a football landed at my feet. I looked up and saw Max standing on the edge of the pitch. He had an uncanny knack of appearing out of nowhere.

I kicked the ball back to him and ran onto my home ground. It reminded me of our very first meeting, except this time he was in a lot of trouble.

'So you think you can play?' he teased.

'Of course I can. Pass me the ball and I'll show you how it's done,' I bantered back.

'Try to take it from me, Zeezou,' he demanded.

I slowly circled him, and then pounced unexpectedly. I dived for the ball with my legs outstretched and managed to kick it out from under him. I was invigorated, surging forward. We lunged for the ball, both of us connecting and falling on our butts. We burst into laughter as the ball continued on its run. It was as though we were the only two people in the world, with nothing to worry about except who would get to the ball first. But then I came back to reality. This wasn't just a kick around, it was serious. I had to know why he took off.

'Max, why did you run away from Bella's?'

'I don't want to go back there. I don't feel comfortable in that place. A couple of days are fine but I can't stand it any longer,' moaned Max.

'But Max, where else can you go? You know that legally you have to stay at Bella's house. Her mama's given her guarantee that you would be cared for and kept out of trouble.'

Max kept picking at the grass while trying to explain himself. 'Lucy, you don't get it. You don't understand my life and what I've been through. I don't need anyone's help. I just want to be left alone.'

'I don't know what you've been through and I don't have any understanding of what it would be like to live on the streets, to have no family and not know where my next meal was coming from,' I said, staring out into the harbour. 'But I do know about isolation and not fitting in, always being the outsider. And I also know that you have friends who care about you and want to help.' I looked into his eyes, doing my best to persuade him.

He looked away. 'I'm used to being on my own. I don't rely on anyone. When someone does something for you they always expect something in return. It's a harsh lesson to learn. I don't owe anyone anything and I know that one day I'll make it on my own.'

'I envy your freedom. But Max, sometimes you have to accept help and believe in those who care about you.

I learnt that when I was abducted. I took my parents for granted. Even though they don't understand me and they drive me nuts, I know they care. That's what gave me the strength to escape from my captors.'

'You have no idea. You've got everything in life. I lost my parents in a car crash. It was awful, even if we weren't always a happy family. I used to run away from home a lot because they were always arguing and my dad was pretty violent. But I still miss them heaps. Football became my saviour . . . it helps me forget about everything. It's my only way out. I don't understand why the hell you're playing, though,' he finished resentfully.

'It's the only place that I fit in, where I can be myself.

It's all I want to do,' I responded vehemently.

'You have it all and to top it off you have one of the best players in the world as your dad. You don't realise how lucky you are. I'd give anything to be in your position.'

'Well Max, you never know your luck. You can meet my papa. I'm sure he'll be happy to help you out. Maybe he could organise a trial for you with one of the clubs. He has lots of football contacts.'

Max looked stunned. Amid the drama that surrounded us, he might have a chance to get closer to his dream.

Before Max could answer, someone yelled out my name from the other side of the pitch.

A lone mysterious figure in a coat and hat, backlit by the moonlight, caught our attention, his foot placed on our runaway football. The shadowy figure stood still, looking in our direction. It was no use running – it was too late. My heart accelerated, but Max was fearless and we stood up and moved towards the man.

'Stop! Don't move any closer. Just look straight at me,' he demanded.

The voice was familiar.

He yelled out more instructions. 'I'm going to kick the ball to you, then I want you to casually run with it straight past me and head towards my car. The police are looking for you and the media is sniffing around. Don't panic, don't rush, just play it cool and we'll be fine. Okay, princess, get moving.'

'Grandpa?'

'Don't talk, just do as I say. Now!'

Max and I obeyed. We raced towards the car and managed to reach it unhindered as sirens echoed through the night. Moments later the driver's door opened and Grandpa slipped inside.

'Grandpa, what's going on?'

'Lucy, couldn't you listen, just this once? I told you to stay home where you're safe. Bella called the house looking for you.'

What? Why didn't she call my mobile? I patted my pockets for my phone and couldn't find it.

'I must have dropped it while we were playing – I have to find it.'

'We don't have time. The police have discovered that Max is missing and they've called a search. Bella's mother is worried about Max and also frightened that her good intentions might backfire . . . She doesn't need any bad publicity, especially with an election just around the corner. Max,' Grandpa turned to him, sitting next to me in the back seat, 'she's very concerned about you and doesn't understand why you ran away. I told Bella I'd look for you. And I'm sorry, but I've promised her that if I found you I'd take you back. I think it's the best way to avoid any further trouble. Lucy, I didn't tell her that you knew about Max's whereabouts. I thought I'd leave that up to you.'

Oh no. I'd upset Grandpa, and now I had to call Bella and explain what'd been happening. I should have told her that I'd found Max. Now she'd be upset with me and would get into a lot of trouble. I'd done the wrong thing by my best friend – how would I make it up to her? And how was Max coping with the fact that he was going straight back to Bella's? I looked at him but he just shrugged and smiled.

As Grandpa pulled up in front of Bella's front gates, Max waved to me and quietly slipped out, disappearing into the night.

When Grandpa saw that he was gone he was furious. 'Houdini has really done it now. His actions will have serious ramifications. That's the mindset of a street kid – act first, think second. I should have warned Bella's mum to be more cautious.'

'But, Grandpa, he deserves a second chance. He's still coming to grips with losing his parents. He has no family, there's no one to catch him if he falls. We've got to help him. I'll talk to Bella and explain what's happened.'

'The locals and I have helped him and cared for him like a second family, but he still finds it hard to trust anyone. There's nothing more you can do for Max tonight. I just hope he's all right. Let's just get inside before any photographers find you,' said Grandpa sombrely.

# Chapter 31

# On the bench

I awoke to a fresh new day, hoping that it would bring some good news about Max.

I managed to feed Gigi and slip down to the shop without disturbing Nanna or my parents. Grandpa, meanwhile, had already made a trip to the markets to buy his stock for the rest of the week. He was setting up the fruit and veggie stands, piling up his produce in colourful pyramids. The store was full of the smell of fresh fruit.

I grabbed an apple and surprised Grandpa with a hug. 'I really appreciate what you've been doing for me. I'm sorry I disobeyed you last night. I'm off to dance class.' I winked, hoping I was forgiven. 'Please tell Mama and Papa that I'll be back in a few hours.'

'I'll do anything for you, but please be careful. You can't help Max any more than you have already. He's very resourceful and will survive this. You just look after yourself, especially after what you've been through. Now get out of here,' he said, giving me a kiss on the cheek.

Dressed in my leotard and trackpants, and armed with my football gear, I headed out to the Reg for my first training session in weeks. I was a little nervous but extremely eager to get onto the pitch and forget about life for a while.

As I stepped out, I noticed the burly security guards across the road watching my every move. There was no going back inside the shop, so I headed up to the church where the dance lessons were held. I couldn't go downhill with the goofy guards on my tail. How could they protect me when they couldn't even stay out of sight? Maybe I could become a spy if my football career didn't turn out, because I'd leave these guys for dead.

When football training was washed out, I'd attended the ballet and jazz sessions. It was good cross-training for football, since it helped maintain my flexibility and strengthened my legs. On this occasion, though, I was merely using the class as a diversion. As I approached the hall, I could see dancers limbering up at the barre through the windows, while Miss Ana counted out instructions. Before I got through the door, I was distracted by a line of ragged-looking men being served food at the adjoining hall. Maybe it was a new soup kitchen – I'd never noticed them before. Or maybe I was just usually too caught up in my own little world.

I walked over to take a closer look and there was Max.

What was he doing there? My heart was pounding so hard it hurt. I was speechless and angry.

After what felt like an eternity I calmed down and found my voice. I decided against yelling at him, since he'd just run off again. So instead of chastising him, I tried to be gentle. 'Max, this is a pleasant surprise.'

'Lucy? What on earth are *you* doing here?' He looked just as shocked to see me there as I was to see him. 'Why are you always stamping around in my territory?'

The men in the line turned their attention to our conversation. I ignored them and focused on Max's big dreamy brown eyes.

'Maybe we just like the same things,' I smartly replied, throwing him a cheesy grin.

He threw a wicked smile back. It was at that moment that I realised I *really* liked him. Of course, this was definitely a secret I wasn't going to share with anyone.

'You wouldn't like this grub,' he said, getting a dumbfounded look from his fellow diners.

I walked closer to him so that we could speak privately. I felt everyone's eyes following us. Standing next to Max, my body was tingling with excitement and all my anger had disappeared. I wanted to hug him and tell him how happy I was to see him.

The food smelt foul. 'You never know until you try . . . but I may have to jump the line, as I'm due at training in about half an hour. It's a shame you can't join me,' I said with a note of sarcasm.

'Ha ha. You couldn't do this every day,' he said cautiously. I felt like he wanted to trust me but wasn't quite sure. 'I'd rather have a choice, and this isn't one of them. What do you feel like today? Fish and chips? Sorry it's not on the menu. You get whatever's going, if anything. Welcome to my life,' he said, extending his arms out to the food trolley ahead.

'How long are you staying here for?' I probed.

'Not long. I'm constantly on the move. The less you know the better.'

'Why don't you go back to Bella and Dylan's house, where you're safe and well looked after?'

'I told you, I can look after myself. I've managed okay on my own for this long, so why get help now?' he said as he moved down the line.

'You don't have to do it on your own and you know it. Why do you push us away? Helen was helping you and it's possible that her position will be at risk once the media get a sniff of the story. Don't you care? Don't you care about us?' I knew I was pressing the issue, but it felt like time Max was confronted about his lack of responsibility.

'You don't understand, Lucy. I've always kept to myself and I've only had to answer to myself . . . me only, just me. I have to look out for number one because unlike you I don't have anyone else. I don't have anyone that loves me, Lucy. There, I said it.'

His eyes became watery, but I could see he was determined not to let the tears flow. He clenched his fists and breathed in deeply. He'd allowed me inside his world without really meaning to.

I didn't know what to say. His words made my heart ache – I couldn't contemplate not being loved, growing up without a family. I instinctively wrapped my arms around him and squeezed tightly. At first he didn't reciprocate, but he slowly succumbed. We held each other gently. I closed my eyes, trying to soak up the moment. I wanted to bottle it and keep it forever. But he soon loosened his grip and stepped back. There was an uncomfortable silence.

Without warning, my mouth sprinted to the finish line. 'It's okay, Max. I'll always be your friend. Lots of people love you, why do you think we've all been trying to help you? When you first went missing, all the locals, the Dunbar Lions and their families were all desperately searching for you. Max, that's love – don't throw it back in their faces.'

He shot me a stunned look. But before he could speak, a volunteer called out that it was his turn in the line.

'What are you having, mate?'

'I'll have it all, thanks,' he replied, as though nothing had just happened.

Just then I heard my name. 'Lucy Zoffi, come on . . . class is about to start. Our concert is at ten o'clock tomorrow. We have a lot of work to cover today and your numerous absences haven't helped. Come on, young lady, get a move on,' ordered Miss Ana, clapping her hands.

'Yes, Miss Ana, I'm coming,' I responded. Great. Now not only the homeless men but also all the dancers were staring at me.

I didn't want to leave Max's side but I had no choice. He shrugged his shoulders and said, 'You'd better go. Hey, don't you have football training?'

'I do. I pretend that I take dance lessons so I can play football. It's a secret. My parents don't know I play.' I blushed. For some reason saying it to Max made it sound silly.

'What? You're telling me that the great Paolo Zoffi doesn't know that his one and only daughter plays football?'

'Yeah, he has no idea about my football life. Only my grandparents know. I make a few appearances at dancing just to stay in touch.'

'That's unbelievable. Football is your dad's life – surely he'd be proud that you play. Why don't you just tell him?' 'It's a long story. For now it's a secret until I'm old enough to leave home and pursue my dream of being a professional footballer.'

'Wow Lucy, I'm really shocked. I thought you had everything.'

'Like I told you before, all isn't as it seems. Look, I have to get out of here, but I can't go out the front door because I'm being watched by security guys. Ever since the kidnapping, I'm under 24/7 surveillance. It sucks!'

I spread out my arms and said sarcastically, 'Welcome to my life!'

'I noticed the security guards across from your grandpa's shop. Don't worry. I can help you.' He smirked. 'I know this church inside out. There's a passageway that leads to the back of the apartment block. Go through there and it'll take you to the Reg.'

'Oh thanks Max, I owe you one,' I said gratefully. 'I think we're pretty much even.'

'Here's my plan – I'll join the class, then fake an injury so that Miss Ana will have to dismiss me,' I whispered.

'I'll come over and help you hobble out, if that's what you want?' he said, treading carefully.

I was excited that he'd offered to be a part of my escape plan. We were working as a team. If only we played together on the pitch . . . that would be something.

'Perfect. But how about you? You're in a lot of trouble. Why don't you come with me?' I asked, hoping for more time with him.

'Lucy, get moving, right now,' yelled Miss Ana. 'Quick, you better go,' said Max. 'Don't worry about

me, Lucy. Just don't tell anyone you saw me, that's all I ask. I'll turn up if I need your help.'

But our little scheme came unstuck. One of the security guards was talking to Miss Ana. It didn't look good, so I grabbed Max and we started running to the back of the building.

'Miss Zoffi, stop,' yelled the security guard as he gave chase.

We kept running. I knew he wasn't going to hurt us: he was here to protect me. Max steered me down a set of stairs and into the bowels of the church. We ran down a passageway and through a door that opened onto the back of the adjoining apartment block.

'We lost him,' Max said casually. 'That was a lot of fun. We'll have to do it again some time. But for now it's ciao, Signorina Zoffi.'

'Max, wait!' I said, but he slipped through the door and was off again before I could stop him. I picked up my bag and headed down to the Reg, elated that I'd made some ground with Max . . . but devastated that he was still running away. When would he stop?

Even though I was distracted and worried, the Reg Bartley Oval, nestled in alongside the moored yachts on the harbour, was a welcoming sight. My team mates were already going through their paces with Coach James as I arrived.

Before I could race off to the toilets to get changed, he yelled out, 'Signorina Zoffi, you're late. Were you out with your boyfriend?' Coach James was always cheeky but this time I was embarrassed at the thought.

'No, Coach James, I don't have a boyfriend. I'm sorry I'm late, I was held up.'

'Oh Zeezou, I was just kidding around. It's great to see you. We're all glad that you're safe and back to play with the Lions. Hey, what kind of football kit is that? I know that we have pink in our strip but that's taking it too far. I thought we'd agreed that leotards and tutus were out this season?' He gave a big grin.

'I've just been to dance class but I, um, I have my gear in my bag, I won't be long,' I stumbled, trying not to give away too much.

'That's okay, I'm just messing about. Now I want to have a wee word about tomorrow's final,' he said, pulling me aside. 'You know that you're one of my best players, but I want to let you know that you won't be starting in the final. I want to ease you back into the team after your absence, and it wouldn't be fair to the boys who've brought us this far and attended all the training sessions to put you straight back in.'

Coach James looked at me carefully, and then smiled kindly. 'Gadi, whom you haven't met yet, has earned his place in the final, so I'll be choosing him to start in your usual position. Please don't take it personally

. . . you're still my shining star, but I've got to be fair to all. Off you go and change into your kit, but don't forget, tutus are out this season.'

I knew he meant well, but I was gutted. I couldn't help but take it personally, even though I knew he was right. It would be good to have some competition, it'd make me lift my game – but my heart sank at the idea that I'd have to prove myself all over again.

I quickly changed into my kit and joined the others on the pitch. Coach James gestured towards a boy I hadn't seen before. 'Gadi, this is Lucy Zoffi, one of our strikers.' 'Hi Lucy. It's nice to meet you. I've heard a lot about you, especially your goal-scoring feats,' he said, as the others looked on to see my reaction.

Gadi took me by surprise with his kind words and his height – or lack of it. He just reached my shoulders, but I figured he probably had very good balance, like many smaller athletes. I was curious to see him in action.

'Thanks, Gadi. Let's hope that between us we enjoy a goal-shooting frenzy.'

I looked over at Harry and Dylan, who were heading my way. 'Where have you been, Miss Ballerina?' Harry asked sternly, as Dylan looked on with fire in his eyes.

'Um, I haven't been well and I lost my mobile. I'm so sorry –' I tried to explain.

Dylan interrupted. 'We've been trying to reach you. Max's disappearance is all over the news. Mum's having a terrible time with the media and her party. They're saying that if she can't look after a street kid how can she look after the state? Wait till I see that ungrateful little . . . He's in for it. Bella's even more furious, since the whole thing was her idea in the first place.'

The team talk couldn't have come at a better time.

'Okay, listen up, enough chitter-chatter. It's great that we have Lucy back in the squad . . . that will give us even more firepower. We've worked hard all season to win the grand final. It's an incredible achievement. I'm so proud of you all!

'To make the final of the Champion of Champions is testament to the fact that you're one of the best teams in the state, if not the best. We've trained really hard over the past few weeks, so we'll just do a light session today. We'll focus on a few set pieces and practise penalties with a quick game at the end. Now that everyone's back it's going to be very competitive for a spot on the team, so give me your best.'

We looked at each other with determined faces. Everyone wanted to start in the final – it was what they'd worked for all season.

I zoned out of Coach James's team talk, preoccupied with Max's situation and my friendships. When they found out that I'd lied about Max's whereabouts, they'd never forgive me.

# Chapter 32

# The pink lion

The training session had gone even better than I'd hoped. It felt so good to be back with the team. Harry and Dylan had still been a little guarded around me, but they'd started to ease up as practice went on. Now I just had to hope I'd get a chance on the pitch today. Luckily, my parents decided that I could continue to stay with my grandparents until our new house was ready for us to move in. They were staying in their luxury hotel up the road, so I pretty much had free rein.

Nanna and Grandpa organised to spend the day with me so that they could secretly watch me play in the final. They even had a little surprise in store.

Gigi came running into the bedroom, jumping up and down on the bed, licking my face. I couldn't help but laugh; she was wearing a knitted blue, pink and white striped dog vest with the Dunbar pink lion embroidered on the top. She looked so cute – she even had pink and blue bows perfectly placed above her ears. My little Dunbar Lions mascot.

'Nanna, Gigi looks so cute. Thanks for going to all this trouble.'

'It's my pleasure. You know that I love to knit and I thought this would be a perfect gift for your first football final here,' she said, beaming.

I was nervous about the game, and about my friends finding out that I'd been in contact with Max. I had to try and block out everything and focus on my football.

I wasn't very hungry, but I made myself eat. I'd need plenty of energy to compete at my best. Nanna had whipped up her special banana pancakes with maple syrup. They were delicious, but I still felt the butterflies fluttering in my stomach. I only managed to eat one serving, while Gigi polished off her bowl. She was excited and ready for action, wagging her tiny tail.

We were just about to leave when the phone rang. Now my stomach was pulsating – the butterflies got worse as I anxiously watched Nanna answer.

'It's your mama, she wants to know what time the dance concert is being held,' said Nanna, giving me a bewildered look.

'Oh, um . . . I can't perform because I'm injured. I pulled a calf muscle playing in the park yesterday, so I can't dance.' Great, yet another lie.

'Did you hear that, Frida? She's injured, what a shame she can't perform. Anyway, we have to go as we're taking Lucy out for the day, but we'll make sure that she takes it easy. Just enjoy your time with Paolo, we'll see you later this evening.' Nanna hung up, looking a little worried.

'Phew. Nanna, you saved me. I don't know how to thank you!'

'It's okay, sweetheart, I understand. One day soon, though, you're going to have to tell them. These little white lies are getting out of hand. I'm sure they'd love to see you play. The sooner you tell them the better.'

Nanna's wise words made me think. Maybe she was right – and maybe if I had her and Grandpa behind me, I'd be able to change my parents' mind?

We finally arrived at the ground. The stand overlooking the pitch was already full of family and friends getting ready for the final. Dunbar's streamers flooded one side of the stand, while the opposition colours of green and white competed for attention on the other side.

Nanna and Grandpa were lucky enough to find two seats in the front row, with Gigi snuggling in on Nanna's lap, looking around and sniffing excitedly. Before I left, Grandpa wanted to share a few words of advice. 'Good luck sweetheart. Go out there and just enjoy yourself.'

Nanna was still impressed with my team's kit. 'Lucy, make that pink lion roar. The costume you're wearing really suits you – such great colours.'

I threw Grandpa a look at Nanna's theatrical description. We shared a little giggle. 'Oh, thanks Nanna and Grandpa. I'm so glad you're here. I'll catch up with you after the game. And be good, Gigi,' I said, beaming with happiness.

While they settled in, I grabbed my bag and headed off to join my team mates in the change room. This time I didn't have to walk out in my tutu – although it was still scrunched into the bottom of my kit bag. It was liberating not having to be so secretive. I was proud to roam around in my Dunbar football gear, especially since I'd been given Zidane's famous number five to wear.

I opened the change room door to a full house. Last again – but this time at least I was dressed and ready to go. There was nothing they could say to stir me.

Standing at the front of the room, Coach James was cool and calm as usual, but he couldn't help himself. 'Welcome Lucy, where's your tutu?' We all laughed.

'Funny you ask, Coach. It's in my bag. I'll get it out so you can try it on. Maybe you could wear it on the sidelines and use it as a secret weapon.' My team mates fell around in stitches.

Coach James unexpectedly grabbed the tutu from me, and put it on over his trackpants for his team talk. Now we were really in hysterics. 'Okay, settle down. This should break the nerves, but it's time to get down to business.

'This is the moment we've been waiting for. We need to all be on our game if we're going to win this match and lift the Champions trophy. Most importantly, I want to see you play good attacking football. Fight for every ball, play as a team and, above all, enjoy yourselves.

'We're up against a fierce opponent, the Hawks. They're a very aggressive team who rattle their opponents with physical strength and good tackles.'

'I can't wait to get stuck into them,' said Jasper.

Coach James nodded. 'Yes, that's what I want, passion and enthusiasm. Now, they have one star player, Amek, who's a big talent, explosive up front and very tall for his age. I think he'll force us to lift our game and that's a good thing. If our defenders can keep him quiet, we'll have a good chance of beating them.'

'Don't worry, Coach James, he won't get past me,' promised Dugald.

'That's what I want to hear. Now, it's been tough choosing the starting eleven, but remember that you'll all get a run.'

This was when my nerves took over.

'Felix in goal, right back Taj, centre back Dugald, sweeper Jonathon – this is a big one for you – left back Jasper, right midfield and captain Brandan, Jared on the left, Morgan and Dylan in centre mid, and Gadi and Harry up front.'

I'd known I wasn't starting but I was still gutted – but so were the other four players stuck on the bench. A part of me had kept a glimmer of hope that I'd be one of the eleven. What made it worse was that they all stared at me, shocked that I wasn't running out with them.

Now my butterflies were raging. I just wanted to get onto that pitch and get a crack at the goal. I broke into a cold sweat and suddenly I had the strangest sensation that the walls were closing in around me. I tried to shake it off, but for some reason I couldn't cope with being in this confined space. I felt as if those arms were grabbing me from behind again; I could almost feel the gun in my back. I had to get out. I ran to the door as I started to hyperventilate.

I could barely hear Coach James's voice because my ears were ringing. 'Lucy, what's wrong?'

I closed the door behind me and sat on the ground, crying. I didn't want them to see me like this.

Coach James leapt over to console me. I was shivering – my body was out of my control. I gasped for breath. He faced me and gently took my hand.

'Lucy, it's okay. Do you need a puffer? It will help you breathe a little easier.' He rummaged through the first-aid kit, then handed me the puffer.

I inhaled from it deeply. I hadn't used one since I was a little kid, but it seemed to help.

'That's better. Lucy don't worry, I'm going to put you on. You're my secret weapon – not the tutu,' he confided, and we shared a giggle.

'It's not about the game. It's the change room – I just felt trapped . . . I'm sorry, I'm so sorry, I don't know what came over me. I couldn't breathe, I just needed some fresh air. I feel much better now.'

'Good, but I think that right now you need to rest. Why don't you stay here and I'll bring the boys out for the rest of the team talk,' he said.

I settled down in the open air, taking deep breaths and trying to work out what had just happened. Harry and Dylan came out and sat on either side of me, trying to comfort me. This wasn't the invincible Lucy Zeezou they knew. I could tell they were shocked to see me in such a vulnerable state.

I had to shake this off and get onto the pitch so I could forget about everything. It had to be related to the kidnapping. Nothing like this had ever happened to me before.

I wasn't the same person any more. Now and then I'd start to feel inexplicably anxious, but it wasn't going to get the better of me. I wasn't a victim, I was a survivor – and I was going to get out there and play my heart out.

'Let's give it everything we've got,' Coach James wrapped up. 'Today is your day, I believe in you, and I know that you can do it. Let's go Dunbar Lions!'

Brandan stepped in. 'Okay guys, let's do our best and fight for every ball. We can win this . . . the championship is ours. Come on Dunbar.'

The atmosphere on the pitch was awesome – our supporters were waving the team's streamers and yelling, 'Let's go Dunbar, let's go!'

But for the first time in my football life I was flat. This was the most important game in my life and I couldn't get excited. I felt detached, even though the boys were on fire – pumped up and ready to take on the world.

Someone started to laugh, and we all turned and looked – Coach James had forgotten to take off the tutu. 'Whoops, it's time this number took a break until we have something to celebrate!' He smiled, quickly throwing off the tutu and putting it in his kit bag.

Tainan, Callum, Hugo, Kurtis and I wished our team mates the best and took our places on the bench. Coach James stayed on his feet, encouraging the boys from the sideline.

I waved to Grandpa and Nanna sitting among the throng of proud parents and friends in the stand. Not my parents. If they saw me here they'd drag me off in shame. The whistle blew and the Lions kicked off, running into the wind. Brandan spotted Harry wide open on the right; he unleashed the ball straight to his feet. Harry accelerated along the line, dribbling up the pitch as free as a bird.

Coach James was very animated, bellowing his instructions from within the designated area. 'Go Harry! Who's helping him?'

Harry crossed the ball into the box to a sea of eager heads, poised to pounce.

'Yours to win, Gadi,' yelled Coach James.

Gadi was the smallest among them but somehow he managed to claim ownership of the ball. He collected it onto his chest, kept it in the air and volleyed it past the defenders and, most importantly, the dumbstruck keeper.

There was a moment's silence as everyone stood in disbelief at the speed and brilliance of the opening goal. Within the first minute we were leading 1–0. The Lions exploded into celebration, jumping up and down, congratulating Gadi on his incredible effort. The boys all piled on top of him to celebrate as our supporters erupted into full song.

Coach James remained calm and cautious. 'Well done Lions, good effort Harry and Gadi, but let's keep up the momentum. Stay focused.'

I was happy for the team, but there went my chance of getting on early – Gadi was lethal up front, very impressive. I'd have do something exceptional to match that performance.

The game gradually settled down, and the rest of the first half became a very tight and tough battle. The Hawks were digging in, determined to level. Eventually, their danger man, Amek, broke free and fired down the middle of the pitch like a steam train.

Coach James yelled, 'Get there Jonathon, come on Dugald, come on, get there.'

And as Amek was about to shoot, Jonathon appeared, throwing himself into the firing line to clear the ball with precision and leave his unsuspecting prey in disbelief.

'Brilliant, Jonathon. That's it. Now turn and face,' demanded Coach James.

But Amek had fallen from the impact, and was clutching his leg while his coach and team mates pleaded with the referee. Jonathon ran back and put his hand out to help Amek up, but he was grimacing and refused his assistance.

'Come on, ref. That's a penalty. He collected him in the box,' yelled the Hawks' coach.

Play was halted as Amek received treatment.

Then I heard Bella yelling from the stands. 'Lucy, I've got to talk to you.' She looked like she was chewing her lip anxiously.

I was astonished that she had come along to watch the game, but so happy to see her. I thought she'd be mad because I hadn't contacted her since Max's disappearance, but at least she didn't look angry with me. We had a lot to discuss, but it was impossible right now.

I was about to yell out to her from the bench when Hugo and I each received a tap on the shoulder.

'Okay, I want you to start warming up. You're going on soon,' said Coach James. 'Lucy, how are you feeling?'

'Oh, I'm ready!' I sprang to my feet with renewed enthusiasm. I gave Bella a shrug and started warming up along the sideline. I couldn't help but wonder what she wanted to talk to me about – it must be about Max. I had to store the distraction away until after the game.

The boys were doing it tough and looking tired as they struggled to hold on to their lead. Hugo warmed up beside me. He was a speed demon

– I think Coach James wanted some fresh legs to lift the pace and regain our momentum.

But before he could make the switch, the persistent Hawks finally broke our defence and came up with a cracking goal to level the game. Of course it was Amek who made the break, sprinting solo like an Olympic athlete and leaving the defenders in his wake. He faced the keeper one on one, and then cleverly faked a turn, easily slotting in the equaliser to make it 1–1.

While the Hawks celebrated their goal – and I had to admit it was classy – the Lions prepared to fight back. Game on!

Coach James called out, 'Ref, substitution. Brandan and Jasper, come off.'

They made their way to our bench to rapturous applause.

'Hugo, you're taking Jasper's position at left back. All I want you to do is stay on Amek. Don't let his size intimidate you. I know you can do the job,' said Coach James, giving him a pat on the back.

'I'll do my best,' said Hugo.

Coach James then turned to me. 'Now, Lucy, you're in the midfield alongside Morgan and Dylan on the right, and you'll wear the captains' armband.'

I wasn't expecting that at all! But I was extremely pleased to be given the honour. It gave me an added incentive to come up with something extra special.

'Play instinctively and make sure you talk to your players. You need to lift them, Zeezou.'

We gave Brandan and Jasper a high five as they left the field. Finally I had my chance!

I ran onto the pitch and lost myself in the sea of Dunbar chants, soaking up the atmosphere. I could feel my energy and enthusiasm coming back. Instinctively, I sprang into a pirouette. One minute I was flying, spinning . . . the next I was landing awkwardly in a heap on the ground. I don't know what came over me. I heard a collective *OOOHHH!* and an eruption of laughter.

Some of the boys sniggered at my fall, while others froze in shock. Oh, nooo! What were my grandparents thinking? Why did I keep doing these crazy things? Great entrance, Lucy.

'Lucy, are you okay?' asked Coach James. I gave him the thumbs up without making eye contact.

I was so embarrassed that I wanted to turn into a crab and crawl under a rock. But instead I stood tall and walked over to take my position ready for the restart. I yelled out as though nothing had happened, 'Come on boys, let's get stuck in. We've got another goal in us before half-time. We can do it.'

While my team mates gathered around me in support, our rivals started jeering.

'Ha, did you forget your tutu, Lucy?' 'Where's your famous dad?'

'Didn't he show you to how to stay on your feet?' 'You don't belong here.'

Harry retorted, 'Shut up. Lucy Zeezou belongs here . . . in fact she's better than all of you.'

I was grateful that Harry had stepped in to defend me, but I didn't want to bite back. And anyway, I'd expected hostility. I just had to stay focused.

The referee blew his whistle. There were just ten minutes left until half-time. We surged forward, driving our way up the pitch, but the Hawks were also getting stuck in, winning the ball back and making a run down the right side. Before they could cross the ball into the box, Dugald slid in and won the ball.

We were unrelenting, creating a way through thanks to Dylan's determination and fancy footwork. He executed a beautiful through ball, which I attacked with vigour, but my run was thwarted. I was winded and cross with myself for losing the ball.

Gadi reclaimed the ball on the run, smartly backheeling to Harry. He cracked it towards the target and our supporters cheered, thinking it was going in, but the keeper got a hand to it.

The ball teasingly hung in the air until it was ferociously put away by Dylan with a superb header into the top right-hand corner.

2–1 to the Dunbar Lions – our supporters roared!

We all ran over to Dylan, embracing him and jumping around, celebrating the hard-earned goal. I took a moment away from the revelry to get a glance at Grandpa and Nanna. I could just spot their proud faces emerging among the throng of pale pink and blue streamers. Bella was sitting next to them but she wasn't cheering. She looked as if she was still in a dour mood. Something was seriously wrong.

The half-time whistle blew and we ran to the change room to grab some drinks and listen to Coach James's instructions. As we ran back out for the second half, our supporters were in full voice. 'Let's go Dunbar, let's go! Let's go Dunbar, let's go!'

The atmosphere on the pitch was just as electrifying in the second half. The Hawks were fighting harder, playing dirty, getting the elbow in at every chance, tugging at shirts and tripping us over. Gadi was their main target, but they slipped up when he was about to receive a cross. A defender came in with a high karate-style kick, missing the ball but striking Gadi on the legs and cleaning him up.

The referee blew his whistle on the spot and signalled a penalty to Dunbar with just five minutes remaining. He gave the defender his marching orders.

Gadi was in trouble, grabbing his right leg and moaning in pain. We gathered around to try and calm him down, but he was suffering. Coach James ran out to inspect his striker.

'Gadi, this doesn't look good. I'm going to have to take you off. Lucy, you take the penalty and play up front for the rest of the game and I'll bring on Kurtis to cover your position in midfield. They're down to ten players, so take advantage of the extra space,' said Coach James.

I really felt for Gadi – he'd been playing like a champion. The moment, though, was mine and I needed to stay calm and focus.

I took my lucky five steps back with my eyes on the ball, focusing on my target. You could have heard a pin drop. I sized up the kick again and just as I was about to move forward, I heard a familiar voice.

'Come on, Zeezou! You can do it!'

At once I felt warm inside yet horrified. What was he doing here? I would have looked around to see if I could spot him, but I was afraid that it would draw unwanted attention to him.

I tried to regain my composure as the referee blew his whistle. I was shaking and distracted. But I had to refocus and strike.

I ran forward and struck the ball as hard as I could, keeping aim at the top right-hand corner. The keeper guessed the right way and parried the ball, but I collected it on the rebound, volleying it into the back of the net to make it 3–1.

I didn't have time to take in the moment – my team mates went crazy, lifting me onto their shoulders, while our supporters' chants echoed throughout the grounds.

Coach James finally unleashed his excitement. 'Brilliant, Dunbar! Brilliant, Zeezou! Great effort.'

But I had mixed emotions, excited that we were minutes away from wrapping up the championship, and yet extremely concerned about Max. And then Dylan and Harry confirmed my fear.

'Lucy, Max is here but we can't see him. We heard him call out to you from somewhere behind those bushes.' Dylan pointed off to one side of the perimeter fence. 'He's history when I get my hands on him.'

'We'll sort him out after the game. Let's wrap it up first and then we'll show him how happy we are to see him,' Harry added sarcastically.

'Guys, calm down. We'll deal with Max later,' I replied coolly, although inside I was panicking.

I looked over to the stands to see my grandparents with Bella by their side and – oh no, it couldn't be . . . how could they come? How did they know I was here?

This must have been what Bella was trying to warn me about. I was in major trouble. My stomach wrenched with fear, my legs started shaking and my eyes fixed on something I'd been dreading for over a year now. If only it was a mirage. I stood there in disbelief, staring straight at them sitting in the stands alongside Nanna and Grandpa.

I couldn't believe it. Papa was casually yet smartly dressed, but Mama stood out like a peacock in her usual glamour-gear. A few photographers and what looked like a television crew scrambled around them, and the spectators were also craning for a look, distracted by the commotion. I couldn't make out my parents' expressions – there were too many people crowding around. Just how much trouble was I in?

Adding to the crazy circus were the burly security guards, who were trying to keep the unwanted media at bay. Could it get any worse?

Right here on the pitch was the safest place for me . . . if only I could stay out here forever.

# Chapter 33

# The letter

'Zeezou! Zeezou, what are you doing?'

Unbeknown to me, the game was well underway again, and I'd just missed a ball that had been kicked straight to me. Harry and Coach James were both yelling at me.

'Come on, Zeezou, we need to keep possession.

Focus!'

But it was too late; the ball was hijacked by the Hawks' tough midfielder, Connor, who found Amek all on his own. The big lanky star striker showed what he could do when he was given too much room. He brushed aside our defenders and effortlessly shimmied around the keeper to score his second goal.

It was 3–2, and with just a few minutes remaining, we had to lift to hold on to our lead. I couldn't concentrate. I desperately wanted to play my best in front of my family and show them where I belonged, but I was terrified of the consequences. I couldn't bear to think about all the lies I'd had told to be here today. I gave them a subtle wave to test the waters and Papa gave me an encouraging nod. That was all I needed. I had a new spring in my step and nothing to lose.

Then I caught sight of police sirens flashing, and two cars pulling to a halt inside the gates next to the stand. The media sniffed a story, and the whole pack broke away from my parents and ran straight over to the police, filming and frantically taking photos.

Bella sprang out of her seat and headed towards the commotion.

The referee had momentarily stopped the game. I took the opportunity to run over to the other side of the pitch in search of Max.

'Hey, are you there? Max, you've got to get out of here,' I said in a low voice, hoping he was close enough to hear.

But there was no answer. What was I thinking? He wouldn't be silly enough to hang around. He was probably long gone by now. I reluctantly turned and started back towards the madness unravelling in front of the dumbfounded players and spectators.

A woman, elegantly dressed in a fitted navy-blue designer blue suit and soft white shirt, stepped out of the second car, along with a small entourage. There was a collective gasp as she stood up and everyone realised who it was. Without hesitation, Bella ran straight into her mama's arms. The press weren't far behind, frantically clicking and firing questions.

'Premier, this is a surprise. We weren't expecting you at a children's football game. Why the unscheduled visit? 'Are you any closer to finding the street kid, Max Spitzer?'

'If you don't mind,' she replied, 'this is a personal visit. I'm here to watch my son, Dylan, playing in his first final. I'm a little late, so please let us be.'

Bella led her mama to the stand without any further obstruction.

The referee blew the whistle to restart the game. Coach James called out, 'Come on Dunbar Lions, focus. It's our game to win.'

We were reaching the dying stages of the match and victory was just around the corner, but it was hard for anyone to concentrate, especially me.

The ball was delivered to my feet. I took it in my stride and manoeuvred around one defender and then another until I was stopped by a heavy tackle and crashed to the ground.

'Get up, Lucy, come on, get up!' screamed Papa.

As I lay there, I looked up and couldn't help but smile as I saw my papa on his feet. Mama grabbed his arm in an effort to seat him but he stood his ground and yelled, 'Come on Lucy! You can do it! You're a Zoffi.' My name had never sounded so good ... Papa was finally seeing me as Lucy the footballer.

Unfortunately, as I got to my feet I could see Amek pound another goal into the back of the net to equalise. The Hawks fans went wild, their green and white streamers waving across the stand, masking our loyal supporters.

The score was locked at 3–3. We had our work cut out to secure victory with just a minute left on the clock.

Spurred on by Papa's support, I found my inner strength. I called the boys into a huddle. 'Come on guys, we can do it. Block everything out and focus. Let's go for the long ball wide to Harry, and then Jared and I will sprint forward together to confuse them for a surprise attack. Dylan and Morgan, follow the play for a possible rebound. Jonathon, stay deep in case they get a break. Everyone else push up. Let's go, Lions!'

Harry and I kicked off and urgently pushed forward to our positions. Dylan and Morgan managed to keep the ball and play it out until we were set. Morgan unleashed a spectacular ball that landed in front of my feet, and I set off to create something special. I ran like the wind but then I heard someone breathing down my neck. I panicked, suddenly overcome by fear. My knees weakened, and the defender easily collected me. I crumbled to the ground again, but this time I felt weakened emotionally. I was distraught that I'd let my team down.

'Come on Lucy! A Zoffi never gives up!' Papa urged at the top of his voice.

The lioness within emerged. I got up and fought for the ball like my life depended on it. I won it back and found Dylan.

He negotiated his way forward, beating all in his path. His efforts drew in a couple of defenders just outside the box. He flicked the ball to Harry, who also attracted a swarm of players. But he played with the ball like a new toy. Outsmarting our rivals, he snuck a pass to our smallest and unmarked midfielder Jared, who unexpectedly unleashed the cracking winner.

Blue and pink streamers came alive once again and shouts for the Lions reverberated throughout the park.

As the final whistle blew I bolted over to the boys and joined in the wild celebration. We had wrapped up the championship with a spectacular 4–3 victory. The boys lifted Jared onto their shoulders, screaming with joy. Coach James ran on to congratulate us, and then pulled me aside.

'Lucy, I'm so proud of you, leading the team to such a magnificent win, especially after your ordeal in Italy. I'm impressed with the way you handled the captain's role, especially while there were so many distractions. I think you have a very big future in football.'

'Thanks, Coach . . . but it's not looking good at the moment,' I said.

'Oh yes it is! A scout from David Beckham's academy wants to talk to you and your family about a possible scholarship. He also has his eye on another player.'

'That's amazing! But I really think my football life is over. My parents are going to put a stop to it. And I can't believe I'm saying this, but I want to stay in Australia.'

'You might want to think about it. I can talk to your parents,' said a surprised Coach James.

'Thanks Coach, but it's time for me to take responsibility and work things out with my parents.'

'Lucy, life is full of surprises and I think that your parents would support you. But right now, I have another surprise for you. Your friend is waiting for you in the change room.'

'Oh?' I was a little confused. Was it Bella with more news?

'Before you run off, please remember that I'm on your side and will do everything I can to help you . . . both of you! Good luck, Lucy Zeezou – you've earned it!'

'Um, Coach? It's not Max is it?' I whispered.

He nodded, and I was filled with excitement. Had Coach James been helping Max all this time?

I rushed off into the change room, but as I neared the doorway I was ambushed by one of those pesky reporters. He launched into Italian-accented English. 'Lucy, do you know Max Spitzer's whereabouts?'

'No.'

'Did you know there are rumours that a terrorist group was behind your kidnapping?'

'No.'

'Why don't you play in a girls' team?'

I was overwhelmed, I didn't know what to say . . . my head was spinning with all the absurd questions he was firing at me. Before I could answer again, Papa came running over.

'What are you doing here? Carlo, I've told you before to leave us alone! You should be in Italy covering the football, not harassing my daughter. Lucy has nothing to say to you. Now get out of here!' Papa sternly demanded. 'You can't threaten me, Paolo. I have a right to ask

questions in search of the truth. It's my job.'

'You don't know what the truth means. Now get out of here,' ordered Papa.

The security guards stepped in and ushered the reporter away. For a moment it looked as though it was going to turn ugly, but he retreated peacefully.

Papa grabbed me and held me tightly. 'My beautiful Lucy, I'll never let anyone try to harm you ever again. I'm so proud of the way you played, even though you've gone against our wishes. I find it hard to watch girls play this sport – it can be so tough, so dangerous. But you've shown me that it's your passion and I understand that.'

My tears subsided and a wave of happiness overtook me.

Papa continued, 'After everything we've been through, how can I deny you the right to pursue your dream when I was given every opportunity to fulfil mine? You play like you belong out there. It would be criminal not to allow you to reach your full potential. Now I know where your Nonno Dino was coming from. He identified and nurtured your talent a long time ago and I must respect that. But I want you to assure me that there'll be no more lies. I will support you, but only as long as we have honesty.'

'Of course, Papa. All I want is your support . . . it means so much to me. I couldn't be happier,' I said.

'Good, that's what I want for you, just be happy. Although you'll still have to convince Mama.' He smiled at me, and relented. 'Maybe you can leave her to me. I think I know how to get her to come around. One thing in your favour is being the face of Love Lucy – going ahead with the commercial will keep her happy and strutting the catwalk with her now and then will help too. Life is full of compromises, Lucy. Believe me, it's give and take. But I can see that you have a fire in your belly which can't be stopped. You remind me of myself when I was a kid.'

'Papa, I've been waiting to hear that for such a long time. Yes, football is my dream, it's my passion. This is the best day of my life! But I have one more thing to sort out. Papa, I need a favour,' I asked.

'Anything,' Papa laughed.

'Will you please give me a minute? I need to catch up with a friend before we leave. I'll meet you soon in front of the kiosk. I won't be long,' I reassured him.

'As long as the guards stay here to make sure you're safe,' he replied, kissing me on the cheek.

'Oh, Papa, please keep them away from me. They're creepy. Can't they watch from their car? Please Papa.'

'Okay, but don't run off anywhere.' He smiled ruefully at me and then walked away.

I nodded and stepped into the change room, full of anticipation. But it was eerily quiet; there was nobody here, just our bags and drink bottles scattered on the floor. Then I caught sight of something white on the back bench – a piece of paper with my name scrawled in red. I picked it up, my heart racing.

Hey Signorina Zeezou,

I knew you could do it. I knew you'd be the winner. Some people are born to be winners, while others have to settle for second best.

I didn't know how to say this to your face, cause I'm not so great with words:

Football is an art form Its players are the artists

Together they have the ability

To transform the canvas into a masterpiece And you are the master with the brush strokes.

Stop at nothing to follow your dream.

I was wrong and you were right . . . you've got to have hope and one day I know you'll make it.

Ciao, Signor Max

I didn't have time to take it all in, because Harry and Dylan raced in. 'Lucy, come on. The trophy presentation is about to start. We're all waiting for you.' As we were about to leave we were startled by a noise coming from the toilets.

'What was that?' said Dylan.

'I didn't hear anything. Quick, we'd better get out there before they start without us,' I urged.

I snuck my treasured letter into my pocket and took one last look around the room. I could see familiar sneakers under the toilet door . . . I paused. I desperately wanted to go to him.

'Lucy, come on, they're waiting for us,' prompted Dylan.

'Oh yes . . . of course.'

We joined the rest of the team on the makeshift stage for the presentation. Bella and Dylan's mama made the occasion more special by handing out the medals to both teams. And then the moment we were all waiting for – she handed me the Champions trophy and we all went wild. The photographers competed for the best shots with the football mums and dads, while the reporters kept a close eye on proceedings, still sniffing for a story. Dylan was thrust into the spotlight. The paparazzo took snaps of him holding the trophy. The premier's son winning his first major competition would probably make the local papers.

My family looked on proudly, Papa as cool as a rock star while Mama gave a perfect smile framed by bright red lips. Nanna and Grandpa were beaming with pride, and Gigi barked happily. This moment was priceless. I'd dreamed of it for so long and today it was a reality.

# Chapter 34

# Betrayal

I'd always believed that football was a matter of life or death. But something in me had changed since I met Max – maybe there was more to life. I had to find him.

Coach James called us all together after we received our medals. 'Lads, Zeezou, there isn't too much to say except that I'm extremely proud. You fought a very brave battle in extremely testing and unusual circumstances. It's great to see all your hard work translate into becoming the state champions. Brilliant, just brilliant!'

Our supporters gave us a raucous round of applause. 'Also, a big thank you to all the parents for all your efforts and commitment to the team. We'll share a toast at our presentation night next Friday.'

To my surprise, Papa stepped in. 'Coach, sorry to interrupt. I'm Pao . . . Lucy's papa.'

Everyone turned to him. Mama stood by his side, her red lips in a demure pout, her eyes concealed by oversized diamante sunglasses, while the photographers took their snaps. How embarrassing!

'Yes, Mr Zoffi, I certainly know who you are. I'm a big fan,' said Coach James. 'I'm glad you and Mrs Zoffi made it to the final. You must be very proud of Lucy.'

'Please, call me Paolo. I'm a very proud papa today. I'm impressed with the way Lucy and the boys played. You have some very talented players in your team. Congratulations.'

I could have died and gone to heaven.

He continued, 'I'd like to invite everyone to celebrate the win tonight at my new favourite restaurant. I'm sure we can enjoy a good celebration.' Papa's invitation was received with shouts of approval from the parents.

My jaw dropped. Papa would usually shun this kind of thing, but he was showing me his full support. This was amazing! I couldn't have hoped for more.

Coach James was also thrilled. 'Paolo, thanks for your generous offer. I think it's a great idea. We all deserve a celebration, and a week is too long to wait.' He winked.

This was such a surreal experience. I was leaving a football ground with a winner's medal around my neck and my parents supporting me. Life didn't get any better than this.

As the parents and players started heading off to the restaurant, Bella and Dylan came over with their mama. 'Hey Bella! Hello, Mrs Jones – I mean, Helen. Thanks for coming to our game. This is my family . . .' I made the introductions.

'It's lovely to meet you all at last. I'm glad to hear that you'll be enjoying Australia for a little while longer. Unfortunately I can't make tonight's celebrations as I have to attend a fundraiser. You must all come over to our house one night for dinner. I'll have my assistant call you to make a time.'

Mama, always the networker, leapt in, 'It's a shame you can't make it but we'd love to come over for dinner, thank you. And we'd love to have your family over in return, just as soon as we move into our new house. Lucy loves spending time with Bella and Dylan . . . I think we'll be seeing a lot more of each other.'

'We'd like that very much. And Lucy, you must alert me straight away if you see or hear from Max. The lawyer has told me that he's in the clear and that no charges will be laid against him, but in the meantime he is supposed to stay with us until the Department of Community Services finds him a place to live. I would have thought that was good news.' Helen gave me a worried smile.

Max was in the clear! I had to find some way of telling him. But I kept a blank expression to avoid any suspicion. 'That's great news.'

We all headed off to our cars. Once we were in ours, Mama unleashed. 'Well, Lucia, what's going on here? You seem to have won the premier's support, but what I want to know is, how could you have lied all this time? I can't believe you've been running around playing football behind our backs and having something to do with a street kid. Why would you betray us?'

'I'm so sorry, Mama, but the one thing that I truly love was denied. You and Papa banned me from playing the game I love more than anything, so it was my only option. It's my dream to play football . . . it's all I want to do, it's where I belong.'

'I've always had such big dreams for you. You could be an international model, admired everywhere you go. I just don't understand. I'm glad that you were being kind to someone less fortunate than yourself, but I'm concerned about your involvement with him.'

Papa joined in. 'Yes, that's a major concern, but I do understand where Lucy's coming from. I know exactly how you feel, Lucy. It's a privilege to know what you want at such an early age. To have a dream and a chance to fulfil it is to have life.'

With Papa's blessing I was able to continue my moment of truth. 'Mama you want me to follow your dream, but it's not for me. I want to live my dream and I hope that you'll support me. Please, Mama, please!'

Her mascara started to run as tears slowly flowed down her perfectly made-up face. She started to blot her cheeks with a handkerchief, but changed her mind and pulled me in for a fierce hug. 'Well, I'll try to understand your choice. I just want the best for you. I thought that you loved modelling. But you looked so happy out there today, just like your papa. How about our Love Lucy campaign, do you still want to do the commercial?' She pulled away and looked at me closely.

'I'm honoured to be the face of the campaign. The commercial will be fun because it's for the family, plus I get to play with the football. It'll be a blast. Just as long as you know that football comes before modelling,' I said with conviction.

That felt good. The truth was certainly uplifting, and it was exciting and reassuring to know that my dream was finally supported by my family – well, nearly. It might take Mama a bit of time to get used to it, but as long as I compromised with a few fashion appearances, it sounded like she might be happy.

But our family bonding session was cut short. We arrived at my grandparents' shop – to the awaiting media. Cameras flashed. The bright lights nearly blinded us as we raced to the front door.

Papa tried to shield us, but they were unstoppable. 'Did you know Max Spitzer has just been found?' 'What do you think about his reconciliation with his uncle?'

Was this true? He'd never mentioned his uncle.

Maybe now he could enjoy a normal family life.

But then they turned on us, starting with the Italian paparazzo Papa had rescued me from.

'Paolo, a well-known Italian actress is claiming that you fathered her son seventeen years ago. Is this true?' 'What do you think about his signing with your club?' 'Lucy, how do you feel about having a step-brother?'

The photographers closed in for shots of our bewildered faces.

We were all shocked at these allegations, especially my parents. Nanna and Grandpa couldn't take it any longer and managed to take shelter inside the shop with Gigi.

Papa's fury couldn't be contained. Without hesitation he grabbed the troublesome Italian photographer and pushed him away. He snatched his camera and threw it to the ground, where it smashed into pieces. A fight nearly ensued when the photographer was assisted to his feet by his peers. He stood facing Papa, yelling at him. But instead of taking a swing, he was more concerned about his camera, screaming with fury and frantically trying to salvage his precious weapon.

Papa roared at all of them in the kind of Italian I can't translate for others' ears. We were horrified to see him lose it, but I wasn't entirely surprised. After all my family had gone through recently, the media had intruded once too often.

Sirens dominated the night air as flashing blue lights zeroed in on the shop's doorstep.

Truth and lies . . . what should I believe? The famous life wasn't what it seemed and now we faced yet another drama. I doubt I'll ever enjoy a normal family life. Just when I thought my life was on track, there was this!

And then a strange thing happened . . . it was as though everyone around me froze on the spot. I stepped out of the crazy scene and was back where I belonged on the football pitch, standing alongside my hero Zizou as we watched my penalty kick hit the back of the net. That sound was so sweet.

*La dolce vita!*

# ACKNOWLEDGEMENTS

I'm grateful to my publisher at Popcorn Press/Fair Play Publishing, Bonita Mersiades, who is also a passionate football fan, for her vision and support in reigniting *Lucy Zeezou's Goal* to give football fans a chance to get to know her as we kick off the 2023 FIFA Women's World Cup in Australia and New Zealand.

I am eternally thankful to the inspiring Former Matildas who also kindly shared their stories and continue to inspire the next generation of footballers which include a Lucy Zeezou fan, the engaging and talented Matildas defender, Clare Hunt, living her dream playing for Australia. Thanks to former Matildas Coach Tom Sermanni for giving me time on the Matildas bench at the SFS and in the sheds for the team talk. What an honour!

Reporting on the 1998 World Cup in Paris consolidated my love affair with football. It's where I experienced the power and passion of the game and its ability to act as an equaliser, bringing together people from all backgrounds, race and religion, chasing the same dream.

Football - its fans and my experiences as a journalist covering the biggest sporting event in the world - has given me the essential ingredients to fuel my story. I feel privileged to have had this incredible opportunity and to share this with you. Massive thanks to all my friends and family whose love and backing has helped me reach my goals.

I'd like to thank the following people:

My dear friend and mentor, former Socceroo and human rights advocate, Craig Foster for his belief in me and treasured coffee catch ups; Tim Bauer for his magical photography; Brenda Dwyer for her friendship and expertise; Marcella Kaspar for bouncing ideas; Amanda L. Tyler and

Charlotte Perry for their encouragement; my colleague at the Australian National University, Andrea Morris for her fearlessness and getting things done; long lunches at Mena Labbozzetta's Italian restaurant, *Figo* and Italy's football legends, Paolo Maldini and Christian Vieri for inspiring the football and fashion combination; my friend and literary agent, Jeanne Ryckmans who is responsible for kickstarting my writing career and supporting my ideas; my nieces and nephews Conor, Lee, Jackson, Riley, Cocoa, Sahara, Brandan, Jared, Jasmin, Daley, Zakk, Khobi, Chase, Zali, and Asha for their encouragement to keep writing;

my amazing in-laws, the late Marie and John Jones for their love and funny tales; my extraordinary late Mum, Jeanette Deep and late Dad, David Deep Snr, who opened my world to endless possibilities and instilled my belief that anything is possible!

I couldn't have done this without my husband Derek, a football tragic and my gorgeous kids now young adults, Dylan and Izabella who are the driving force behind my Lucy Zeezou series.

Finally, a huge thanks to all my Lucy Zeezou fans. I'm forever grateful for your love and encouragement to create more stories. I hope Lucy inspires you to follow your dreams.

# ABOUT THE AUTHOR

Liz Deep-Jones is a published author, journalist, producer, presenter, film maker, curator and the inaugural Freilich Arts/Media and Activism Fellow at the Australian National University in Canberra. Her best-selling young adult novels, *Lucy Zeezou's Goal* and *Lucy Zeezou's Glamour Game* have been re-released for the upcoming 2023 FIFA Women's World Cup in Australia and New Zealand. Liz is passionate about football as it breaks societal and race barriers and is a champion for human rights, inspiring young people to take action through her mentoring role at the ANU in media and arts activism. The proud Sydney-sider is travelling her *We Bleed The Same* anti-racism exhibition and documentary across Australia. She's also writing her third novel, hoping to inspire young readers to never give up on their dreams.

# MORE REALLY GOOD FOOTBALL FICTION FROM POPCORN PRESS

Jarrod Black
Chasing Pack

Anna Black
This girl can play

The End of the Game

The Gaffer

Game

The Yawning Giant